Dream Away

Sunrise

A Psychological Novella of Horror

By Mike Rivera

Dream Away Sunrise

Acknowledgment

I owe a special thanks to my wife, Amanda, for keeping me moving toward the finish of this book and for her insight on the final draft, even though she had little idea of what I was creating at the start.

I am grateful to my mother-in-law, Deb, my mom, Karen, and my sister-in-law, Dez, for taking the time to read and review this work. To the family members who knew I was up to something and kept checking in, asking if it was finished yet—thank you for the gentle push.

And to friends and co-workers who supported me when I finally broke the news, your encouragement helped me cross the finish line.

Table of Contents

Chapter One:
Eddie (The Life He Built)

Eddie sat at the kitchen table in his Henryetta, Oklahoma home, his fingers tracing the freshly revealed wood grain. A testament to his careful handiwork. As he admired the smooth finish, his gaze drifted past the wide windowpane, not truly seeing the fluttering leaves, the darting birds, or the occasional passerby. His thoughts, as usual, pulled him under.

He wasn't quite middle-aged—not yet. But his skin, weathered like old leather, told the story of a man who had lived through more than most. Hinted at a life shaped by hard work—and perhaps a few lingering regrets. Or maybe it was the recent shifts in his world? The weight of everything that had happened.

For years, Eddie had been the foreman at a ranch in Okemah. At the Ranch, his cowboy hat was as much a part of him as his dark brown leather vest, his western-cut plaid shirt, blue jeans, and tan canvas boots.

Off the ranch, you might not have recognized him. In his own time, Eddie dressed in quiet dignity—always sharp. A Trilby hat, a black shirt under a matching vest, black flannel dress pants, and two-tone black-and-brown shoes. He was the kind of man who took pride in how he presented himself, no matter the occasion.

After years of careful saving, he had moved to the foothills up on Lake Road just above Nichols Park in Henryetta. Far enough out that the nearest neighbor was a thirty-five-minute drive, more than just another ranch away. His home was rustic, perfectly suited to him. Its weathered gray walls, with their natural wood grain, spoke not of neglect but of intention. He liked things that told a story.

The two-story house, roughly a thousand square feet, had a wide porch supported by arched wooden beams he'd crafted himself. Wind chimes hung from the rafters, their occasional notes whispering secrets into the breeze. Two dark wood rocking chairs flanked the front door, facing the drive where an old pickup sat parked beside a stretch of open field. Nearby stood a woodshed, stacked high with fresh-cut lumber, and a well-used workshop large enough for projects like the table he'd just finished.

Inside, a grand oak door with cherry inlays—one of Eddie's finest works opened into the living room. It wasn't extravagant, but it was thoughtfully arranged: a comfortable couch, a recliner, a modest TV, and a radio tucked neatly in the corner. The kitchen had the same old-time charm—a wood-fired stove, a vintage water pump faucet, and a percolator coffee pot resting beside powdered creamer and sugar. An old, yellowed refrigerator hummed softly. And of course, the wide glass window framed the very table he'd just restored—rescued from the ranch and brought back to life. Three mismatched chairs surrounded it, each with its own quirks and character.

At the back of the house, a grand staircase climbed to two bedrooms separated by a shared bathroom. The larger, naturally, was Eddie's. It was as tidy as the rest of the house. One nightstand held framed pictures—a silent gallery of memories. The other, a lamp, his watch, and a simple clock.

The smaller bedroom told a different story. Not messy, exactly—just lived-in. A single bed, a small closet, and a nightstand with a lamp. The room had a quiet energy, like it was waiting for someone. As you walked through the home, the order and cleanliness were impossible to miss. Everything had its place. For a man like Eddie, that meant something. The neatness didn't feel like routine. It felt like ritual.

Eddie was a quiet man now. A man of few words, people would say. But that hadn't always been true. Just a few years back, he'd been full of fire and stories. Give him a couple of drinks, and he could talk your ear off. He was the talk of the town—in the best way. The kind of man people relied on. The kind of man you could take home to meet your folks.

And once, someone did.

Yes, Eddie had been married once.

It was early in his days at the ranch. He used to make regular supply runs into town for Vinnie, Eddie's boss. One day, while crossing the street toward the general store to pick up a sack of feed, he saw her—Caroline. The prettiest woman he had ever laid eyes on.

He had seen her before, of course, but always in the back area of the store— somewhere he never had reason to go. Until that day.

Chapter Two:
Caroline (The Woman He Loved)

Caroline— not to be confused with Carolyn—never let anyone get her name wrong.

"No, it's Caro-LINE!" she'd correct, polite but firm. She'd been teased in grade school by kids who deliberately mispronounced it, and even as an adult, strangers on the phone made the same mistake. It always made her cringe.

In many ways, Caroline was refined. Her appearance was impeccable. Her hair, never out of place. Her clothes, neat and elegant. Charming, sweet, and composed, she also didn't take lip from anyone—especially not from a man. To the men, she was a tough nut to crack. To the women, she was the most organized and gracious person in town.

Though she didn't come from wealth, she carried herself with grace. On her days off, she wore a matching polka-dot hat and scarf with a Jean Patou-style suit—the kind Jackie Kennedy might have chosen.

At work, she favored a blue velvet crescent hat with a soft tea-length dress—modest, but stylish.

For years, Caroline owned Hotchpot Depot in Shawnee, Oklahoma, the town's general store. Her store was immaculate—everything had its place. People came from miles around for groceries and ranch supplies.

Born and raised just a few blocks away, Caroline knew everyone and everything—not because she was nosy, but because she had a gift for making connections. People liked her. She had a warmth that drew others in.

That's what happened with Eddie.

He'd been making regular supply runs to her store for the ranch where he worked. There was something about him—a quality no other man seemed to have. He wasn't flashy. As far as she could tell, he always wore his work outfit. But he was genuine. Steady. Warm in a quiet kind of way. After a few conversations, a spark lit between them. A few dates later, that spark deepened into something more. Within the year, they were married.

"Now there's true love!" People would say when they saw them together.

After the wedding, Caroline moved in with Eddie. At the time, he was living in a run-down cabin provided by the ranch. It lets him be close to work. As a foreman, his job mostly involved overseeing the crew and keeping things running. But sometimes, he'd get called out late at night—to chase off coyotes, foxes, and even the occasional wolves threatening the livestock.

Caroline adapted to ranch life quickly. Not long after settling in, she became pregnant. As her belly grew, the ranch hands treated her with the same respect they showed Eddie.

She continued working at Hotchpot Depot until she was eight months along, finally stepping back to let someone else manage the store in her final month.

When the baby arrived—a healthy, beautiful boy—Caroline and Eddie, they couldn't have been happier.

He had her bright eyes and his father's dark hair.

A few months later, Caroline eased back into part-time work at the store. Eddie and the ranch hands took turns watching their son. It became a village effort.

Eventually, the couple bought a house of their own. It was a fixer-upper, but Eddie had a knack for carpentry. He'd already transformed the old cabin into something cozy, so this new project didn't faze him.

His buddies from the ranch stopped by

to help, share beers, watch some TV, and enjoy Caroline's home-cooked meals. Meanwhile, Caroline took charge of the inside of the house—unpacking boxes, arranging furniture, and keeping everything spotless. It was no small task, especially with a toddler tracking mud through the halls and scattering toys everywhere. Still, she met the challenge with grace.

As their son grew older, the domestic chaos lessened. His toys mostly stayed in his room.

Caroline began to contemplate leaving the store for good. The 30-mile commute wore on her, and their son increasingly needed her at home. She'd done her time, built her reputation, and was ready to fully embrace her role as a mother and wife.

Chapter Three:
Joey (The Boy He Loved)

Born on April 26, 1949, Joey inherited his mother's bright blue, observant eyes and his father's thick, dark hair. From the moment he could toddle, his early years unfolded on the family ranch—a tapestry of carefree wonder.

His days were often painted in red plaid and blue denim, chasing squawking chickens across the sunbaked yard or tumbling in the dirt with the ranch dogs. A perpetual whirlwind, he would be marked by the badges of childhood: A smear of mud, the shine of a freshly conquered puddle, or the tell-tale dusting of chicken feathers clinging to his clothes.

As soon as his legs were long enough to keep up, Joey became a fixture among the ranch hands. They welcomed him with good humor, charmed by his relentless curiosity. "Why?" Was his favorite refrain—spoken with wide-eyed sincerity—as they patiently showed him how to feed the livestock, fix a sagging gate, or mend a stretch of fence.
He absorbed it all. His young mind was a

sponge for the rhythm and wisdom of ranch life.

At home, Joey split his time between the dusty corrals and the bustling aisles of Hotchpot Depot, where his mother worked. There, he became a familiar, beloved presence.

Locals and out-of-towners alike were drawn to him—he had quick wit and a sharpness that surpassed his years. More than a few customers had remarked.

"You've got a mighty fine boy there, Miss Caroline."

To which she would always beam with pride and reply,

"Why, thank you!"

The year Joey turned eight—1957— marked a significant change: The family moved into a house nestled in the foothills. It was, by all accounts, a fixer upper. But Eddie, ever the visionary, saw only potential.

Caroline, ever pragmatic, didn't object. Her only stipulation: it would eventually be clean, orderly, and livable. Eddie was already brimming with plans.

"Joey, see over there?" Eddie pointed across the patchy field, where weeds grew tall and wild. "That's where I'm going to build my workshop. Everything we need for this house—gonna build it right there. I can't wait."

Joey's eyes followed his father's gesture, but his attention drifted back to the house. Something about it didn't sit right with him. A cold unease curled in his gut, and he couldn't explain why.

"And right next to that'll be the woodshed!" Eddie continued, grinning widely. "Just like at the ranch. Cutting wood for us this time, not for Vinnie."

Joey wasn't smiling. His lips pressed into a hard line... He stared hard at the house.

"Dad... Can't we live somewhere else?" He asked quietly, barely above a whisper. "I don't think I like it here."

Eddie blinked, caught off guard. "Why, son? This is a great house! Just needs a little elbow grease. You'll see—once I'm finished, you're gonna love it." He gestured toward the empty space in front. "See this? No porch yet, but I'll build one—with curved beams. It'll be modern, but classic. Just what your mom wants. Right, honey?" He called.

But Caroline was already inside, unpacking boxes with her usual focus.

Joey sighed. "Guess we'd better help her before she starts hollering at us."

Eddie chuckled. "Yeah, I guess you're right, son."

Joey didn't want to go inside. But back then, kids didn't argue. You did what you were told. So, with a heavy heart, he followed his father through the threshold.

Inside, Caroline was already knee-deep in the living room—sorting through boxes like a force of nature.

"So, Joey, how was school?" She asked, muffled as she pried open a cardboard flap.

"It was okay." As he dragged another box across the floor.

"Did you make any new friends?"

"I played with a new kid who just moved here."

"That's good, sweetheart!" She said without looking up.

As they worked, Joey caught a flicker of Eyes fixed on the landing. But he saw nothing more. He dismissed it—probably just his dad. A moment later, Eddie stepped out of the kitchen behind him. Joey jumped!

"Dad, weren't you just upstairs?"

"Nope. I was just putting stuff away in

the kitchen. Why?"

Joey turned slowly, pointing toward the stairs.

"Oh... I thought I saw you walking up there."

A cold, prickling chill crept down his spine. He was sure—absolutely sure—he'd seen someone. And it wasn't any of them.

By dusk, a semblance of order had been achieved. Half the house was unpacked, and the bedrooms were ready for their first night.

But Joey didn't sleep well. He barely slept at all. Maybe an hour, tops. He couldn't shake the feeling—something was watching him. And then, deep in the suffocating stillness of night, he heard it: A woman's scream. Distant. Sharp. Aced with unimaginable pain.

Chapter Four:
The Moments of New Beginnings
April 26, 1957

*E*ddie stirred, a sound, indistinct at first, growing louder.

"Dad... Dad! DAD!" Joey's shouts finally pierced his sleep.

Still groggy from the previous day's labor, Eddie lifted his head from the pillow, tilting it slightly. With one eye cracked open, he heard it again.

"Dad!"

"Um... oh, hi, son!" Eddie mumbled, his voice thick with sleep. He propped himself up on the bed. "What's wrong?" He saw the stark fright on Joey's face.

"It's Mom!" Joey's voice was severely nervous. "Something's after her! Come on!"

Eddie was out of bed in a flash. "Where is she?"

"She's in the woodshed! Something's attacking her!"

Eddie bolted down the stairs and dashed to the door. He flung it open. Outside, a heavy darkness pressed in, eerily quiet—no wind, no crickets.

"Stay inside!" Eddie commanded.

He rushed towards the shed. Inside, Joey panicked, unable to see what was happening. Suddenly, he heard a crash, like a door being ripped from its hinges. Then, heavy, running footsteps pounded towards the house. Freaking out, Joey huddled just off to the side of the door. He heard screams – they sounded like his mom.

Then, Eddie yelled! "No! Stay back!"

The fast, heavy stomping thundered onto the porch, echoing the sound of his dad's boots. Eddie blasted through the door, running at full speed. Before he could turn to slam it shut, Joey caught sight of his mom, coming quickly after him. Behind her, the most terrifying figure he had ever seen materialized. It was dark, wispy black smoke trailing from its form. Its head and body peered around the corner of the shed, its hands pulling itself from within. The head bore massive black horns, curling back from the crown, and the brightest, most piercing red eyes that burned through the night. Its body looked like the burning bark of a cottonwood tree. The smoke smoldered from the creature into the air—yet there was no smell. As the creature emerged from the shed, Joey's eyes met its fiery gaze, chilling him to the core. Was that a demon? He wasn't sure what he'd just seen.

Eddie slammed the door shut.

"But Dad! Mom's outside! Open the door!" Joey screamed.

Eddie looked at his son, his face a mask of sheer terror. "Son... your mom is..." Eddie struggled for words, breathless. "Your mom... it's not her! She's been possessed by that... thing... that monster. Whatever she is now, she's not your mother anymore."

Caroline's voice, deep with a demonic tone, resonated from the door, her banging rattling the wood and making it creak. "Eddie... Joey... it's okay, it's just me, Mom. Can you just let me in? I swear, there's nothing to be afraid of... Will you please let me in?"

Eddie and Joey in shock; disbelief etched on their faces.

"Dad? What was that in the woodshed? Behind Mom? I saw its eyes... those horrible red eyes, and it's all black and smoking. Dad, was that a demon?" Joey asked nervously, tears streaming down his face.

Eddie peered through the corner of the window, trying to see what was happening outside. He whispered, "Shhh. Quiet now... I don't know. I don't know what that was. But I know it wasn't human... it took her over."

"What happened out there?" Joey pressed.

"I saw your mom in the woodshed, just standing there, not moving, looking away from me. It was dark in there, and the only light I could see was this weird red glow. It looked like your mom was staring at it." His father shivered, goosebumps rising on his arms. "I called for your mom, but she didn't say anything. I called again, 'Honey! Are you okay?' No reply, only she turned her body towards me. Her body creaked as she turned. Her eyes were black, with no signs of white. The creature behind her stood up to see me."

"You will join me. There is no running away from this. You... will... join the Horde of darkness and the dead!" Caroline's voice deepened, dark lines beginning to form on her face as she lunged at him.

"That's when I yelled, 'Stop!'" Eddie recounted. "I started out of the woodshed; she was following me. I slammed the door, but the creature tore it off its hinges."

"She was coming at me. I told her no, to get back. She lunged, trying to grab the back of my shirt. I ducked, looked back at her face, all covered in those lines. While I was looking back at her and walking backward, I tripped over the axe on the log. She reached down and grabbed me, and as her hand closed on my arm, it started burning. I let out a yell like I'd never done before."

Eddie felt something strange, something unreal. He looked at Joey, uncertain of what was happening. He started to shake and tremble, a look of sheer terror in his face and eyes. Was he turning into a demon?

Suddenly... Eddie awoke. Caroline was in bed beside him, shaking his arm gently. "Shhh, it's okay... it's okay, honey, shhh, it's okay! It's just a bad dream. You're okay now, it was all just a bad dream!" Caroline soothed.

Confused and dazed, Eddie stammered, "What? ... What? ... What happened?"

"It's okay, you were having a nightmare!" She repeated.

"Oh my God! I... what a bad dream I had. You were possessed by some sort of demon, and he was behind you in the woodshed. It scared the hell out of me!"

"I'm sorry, honey. That sounds horrible! Do you want me to get you something? Some water, perhaps?"

"No nothing, I think I'll be okay. Thank you anyway!"

Joey shuffled into the room, still groggy.

"Mom, Dad, what's going on? I heard Dad screaming."

"It's okay, little bear," Caroline replied. "Dad just had a nightmare, that's all. He's okay. Just go back to bed."

"Oh, okay, Mom. Can you get me some water, please?"

He hadn't had to ask his parents for water in years; he could usually get what he wanted on the darkest nights. But in this old, new house, with the feeling of being watched all night, he didn't dare go downstairs. Plus, the figure he thought he saw at the top of the stairs that evening scared him even more just thinking about it.

"Of course, little bear, I'll be right there. Just go back to bed, I'll bring it to you in a minute."

"Okay, Mom, thanks!"

He heard someone walk out of his parents' bedroom, unsure who it was.

"Joey, son, is that all you want? Just water? Did you want anything else?" Caroline called.

"Just water. Thanks, Mom!"

He heard her walk down the stairs. Then, movement from the bedroom across the hall, followed by footsteps approaching his room.

"Son?" His dad's voice inquired.

"Yes, Dad?"

His dad entered the room. "Sorry, son, about that earlier. I had one hell of a nightmare. I'm sorry if I scared you." Eddie chuckled.

"It's okay, I understand."

"How's your night going? Are you sleeping well, besides me screaming in the middle of the night?" Eddie chuckled again.

"Not really that good... I think it's being in the new house and hearing different noises." Joey offered, though the creaking and popping of the house were the least of his worries. He was more afraid of what had been watching him, the impenetrable darkness outside, the absence of stars and moon, and the dead silence of the night.

"Oh, I'm sorry. Well, just give it a few days. I'm sure you'll find our new home just fine and be able to sleep like a bump on a log."

They both heard the creaking and popping of the stairs as Caroline ascended.

"First thing I do with this house is replace those steps after I get my workshop built!" He commented.

Seconds later, Caroline rounded the

corner and entered the room with a glass of water.

"Here you go, baby bear."

"Thanks, Mom!"

"You're welcome. Now, drink up and go back to sleep. It's going to be morning soon enough."

"I'll see you in a few hours, son. Best get your sleep; we've got a lot to do tomorrow. And some of the guys will be coming over soon as they finish their morning duties." His dad said.

They both left the room, one of them turning off the light and closing the door behind them. They returned to their bedroom and went back to sleep.

The morning arrived with the sunrise. Around 6:30 AM, Caroline and Eddie both rose. Caroline headed downstairs to make breakfast, then planned to prepare lunch for the arriving crew before leaving for her own work.

Eddie dressed, bracing for a hard day of breaking ground for the workshop, which he estimated would be about ten feet by twenty feet when finished. As he walked past his son's room, he paused, listening. Behind the door, he heard Joey still sleeping. Normally, he would wake his son, but decided to let him sleep until breakfast was ready. After all, Joey had worked hard yesterday, moving and unpacking boxes for his room, not to mention his restless night. Eddie headed downstairs, joining his wife as she prepared breakfast.

"Do you need any help, sugar?" He asked, reaching for a coffee mug.

"In fact, yes, if you don't mind, I'm just going to make some quick sandwiches for you boys. If you work on that instead, I'll finish breakfast...Where is Joey?"

"He's still sleeping. I decided to let him sleep until breakfast is almost ready."

"Oh, okay." Continuing with breakfast.

Eddie called up to Joey. "JOEY! Breakfast time! Come and get some!"

Minutes later, footsteps sounded on the stairs. Joey, still half-asleep in his pajamas, shuffled into the kitchen for breakfast.

"Morning, Mom, Dad." He mumbled.

"Good morning, kiddo!" said Dad.

"Good morning, my sweet little bear!" Mom exclaimed.

"Sit down, have some breakfast." Dad said.

Joey sat at the table and ate his eggs with milk. Caroline finished in the kitchen and got ready to head to the store. Eddie, after helping his wife with breakfast and lunch prep, sat at the table and then cleaned up the kitchen after eating.

"Joey, head on up and get ready for the day!" Eddie told him. "The guys will be here soon, and we'll need your help today. And if you work hard, I'll let you go with your mom tomorrow when she goes to work so you can have fun in town with your friends. But help your mom first if she needs it, okay?"

"Okay, Dad, I will."

Joey headed upstairs to get ready. Eddie stepped outside to uncover the bags of concrete. He then walked over to the truck, pulling out shovels and laying them on the ground where they would be working. *The guys should be here any time now,* Eddie thought. He walked back into the house to check on his son.

"Joey! Are you ready yet?" He yelled up the stairs.

"Almost! I'll be down in a minute!" Joey yelled back.

"Okay, well, hurry up! I'll need your help as soon as you're done!"

Eddie returned to the truck, moving saws to the back while he waited for his son. Joey finally emerged from the house.

"What can I help you with?"

"Come here, help me move the saws off the truck, and we'll put them over there with the shovels."

They got everything moved and set up. "Now, son, let's get the lumber uncovered." They walked over to the lumber pile, uncovering the planks of wood.

Eddie and Joey heard the rumble of a truck approaching. It was the men, as the truck came up the road, both Eddie and Joey took a break, waiting by the truck for them. The vehicle rumbled to a stop beside them.

"Morning, boss man! Joey!" The men called from the truck.

"Morning, guys! Are you all ready to get to work?" Eddie asked.

The six men exchanged glances. One spoke for the rest. "Yeah, boss, let's get to it! Let's take a break once we get the four walls up for your work shed."

"Alright then, guys, thanks for the help and your time! I couldn't do all of this on my own in any good time." Eddie stated.

Eddie turned to Joey. "Can you go inside and start bringing us all a glass of water? After that, you can do your chores. Check in on us every now and then; I know we'll need your help."

"Sure thing, Dad! I'll be out in a flash with the waters!" Joey ran inside.

As Joey started to walk into the kitchen, he caught a glimpse of a man standing at the top of the stairs out of the corner of his eye. He took a few steps backward, out of the kitchen, and looked up the stairs, only to see nothing. He heard nothing —no running water, no footsteps, nothing at all. He brushed it off as his imagination and headed back into the kitchen to fetch water for his dad and his buddies. He ran out with the first set of water and started back in for the next. Again, as he entered the kitchen, out of the corner of his eye, he saw the man, this time on the steps descending. Joey stopped dead in his tracks and quickly looked back to find no one there. The hair on his neck stood on end, goosebumps rising on his arms. He stood still for a few moments, then headed into the kitchen for the second round of water.

Moments later, he emerged from the kitchen with two more glasses, slowly walking to the front door, his eyes fixed on the stairs the entire time. He delivered the water to the next two guys but now had to go back in for the last two. He started back inside the house, this time watching the stairs as he went into the kitchen, seeing nothing. Joey quickly grabbed the last two cups of water and started back to the front door, watching the stairs again, only to see nothing. He made it to the front door, and as he turned to look at the knob, he saw the figure of a man at the bottom of the stairs. Joey jumped and fully looked to where he had just seen the man, only to find nothing in sight again. Joey ran out of the house, thanking God he had nothing left to do inside and all his chores were to be done outside. He delivered the drinks.

"Thanks, son!" His dad said, and the guys all echoed the sentiment.

Joey did his chores, and halfway through, he decided he'd better check in with his dad.

"Dad, how's it going?"

The workshop was about half done. They had managed to get all four walls up, and the guys were ready for lunch.

"We are doing good, son, but it's stopping time; it's time for lunch." Eddie replied.

"Guys, break time! Come on in and grab some lunch." Eddie told his crew.

"Joey, come on in, help me get the food

out for everyone." Eddie instructed him.

Joey still hadn't mentioned anything about the man he kept seeing, keeping it to himself.

They all went inside. A few lingered in the living room, and a few went into the kitchen. Everyone sat down to eat, but no one had seen any sign of the man Joey kept seeing. He had been hopeful that someone else would have seen him, but not a word came from anyone. It made him think he was going crazy.

"Alright, guys, wash your plates, and let's finish this up. I'm sure we'll be done by the end of the day. Joey, come on out when you're done." Eddie told him.

Eddie washed his plate, and the men lined up behind him. One by one, they walked out of the house, grabbed their tools, and went back to work. Joey chipped in and helped wherever he could.

By 5:00 PM, they were almost done. They all heard a car driving up the road towards them. They kept working until the car got close enough to see. They all paused and waited. It was Caroline, coming home from work. Eddie got down off the roof, and Joey came out to meet her as she pulled up. She came to a stop next to the trucks, and Joey ran up to her.

"Hi, Mom!" He said.

"Hi, little bear!"

"Hi, honey! How was your day?" Eddie asked.

She looked around as she spoke. "Hi, honey! It was a good day. It was busier than normal, so that was great! I see you guys are almost done with the workshop. Hi, gentlemen! Great job! Looks great!" She replied to Eddie and the men.

"Evening, Ma'am. Thanks!" The men replied.

The guys turned their attention back to working on the shed as the end was nearly in sight. Eddie walked Caroline to the house. Joey stayed with the crew to help finish it up. Eddie came back out moments later.

"Hey, guys, the missus wants to know if you all want to stay for dinner?"

The guys looked around at what was left to do, then talked amongst themselves. One replied, "Nah, Sir. I think we will finish this up and head out before it gets too late. Phill's driving and doesn't like that canyon all that much. But thanks for the offer, though."

"Well, thank you all for your help! Before

you leave, I have something for all of you guys for helping, so make sure to check in with me beforehand." Eddie replied.

Eddie started picking up unused tools and putting things away. Joey helped, and the guys finished up. Eddie ran into the house and called for Joey to come help. They both emerged with cases of beer, one for each guy, and loaded them into the truck.

The men all joyfully exclaimed. "Thanks, hoss! Much appreciated!"

Caroline came back out of the house. She thanked the men and wished them safe travels before they headed off down the road.

The family returned inside for the night; they ate dinner, and Joey headed off to bed just afterwards. On his way to the stairs, Joey felt a cold spot, and the hair on the back of his neck stood on end. He walked briskly, reaching the stairs and running up them to the bathroom. He was getting ready for bed, taking a bath, and brushing his teeth. The mirror in front of him offered a clear view of the hallway, and from time to time, he glanced behind him, only to see nothing. He headed off to bed, awaiting his mom and dad to tell him goodnight and give him his nightly kisses on his forehead. He heard footsteps coming up the stairs. He was nervous as to who it could be, but it was only his parents coming to tuck him in. They soon left for their bedroom, looking forward to a good night's sleep after a long day at the store and working on the workshop. The lights went out, and everything was once again silent.

Chapter Five:
The Visit
August 9, 1957

A few months had passed. The workshop was long completed, and now Eddie slowly chipped away at the woodshed, taking his time, knowing he had until the first snowfall. It had been a busy season at the ranch, and the store was thriving, nearly doubling last year's sales.

Joey, still on summer break, split his time between helping at the store and the ranch, fitting in moments with friends whenever he could. Yet, an unease clung to him regarding the house. He still caught glimpses of the shadowy figure, always just out of the corner of his eye, never directly. Lately, these sightings have become more frequent. The figure remained passive, and Joey, despite his growing fear, kept it secret from his parents, only hinting at it to his best friend from time to time.

Now, to the present day, and it would prove to be quite a day indeed.

At the ranch house, Eddie sat in Vinnie's office, discussing daily duties. Through the window, he could see a few of the men in the welcome area outside. From his chair, across the desk from Vinnie, both had a clear view of the road leading into the ranch—a perfect vantage points for comings and goings. Their conversation halted abruptly when black-and-white vehicles, patrol cars, kicked up dust as they approached. Four cars rolled to a stop, and workers scattered across the yard paused their tasks, watching uniformed men step out. FBI. They began walking purposefully toward the ranch house door.

Eddie, Vinnie, and the others watched them approach. Eddie's eyes landed on one of the agents—Bill, his high school classmate. A knot formed in Eddie's stomach. *Why was Bill here? Who were they after?* The agents opened the door, asking for someone, though Eddie couldn't make out the name. He watched as a worker pointed in his direction. The agent turned, gave the worker a nod of thanks, and then, with his colleagues, walked directly into the office.

"Wow, Bill, I can't believe you're here!" Eddie exclaimed, rising. "I haven't seen you in years! How are you? Why are you here? You're FBI? I can't believe it!"

"Hi, Eddie. I've been good." Bill replied,

his expression solemn. "Yeah, I'm FBI. I've been at it for about ten years now. And as for why I'm here, Eddie... well, I'm here for you. I'm sorry, but you have to come with us."

"Wait... what? Why me?" Eddie questioned, bewildered.

"Sir, what has he done?" Vinnie interjected.

"Sir, that is none of your concern." Another agent stated firmly.

"Eddie, I'm sorry to do this here and now, but I need you to turn around and put your hands behind your back" Bill instructed.

Eddie complied, turning slowly. Bill cuffed him, then led him out of the house. The men in the yard stood in stunned silence, watching as Eddie was escorted to the cars, all wondering what on earth Eddie could have done to warrant the FBI's attention. They placed Eddie in a vehicle and drove away.

The drive from outside of Okemah to Oklahoma City took over an hour and thirty minutes. By the time they reached downtown, it was just past noon. Eddie noticed they were heading to a familiar area. The agents made a final turn into a small strip mall. Eddie realized he had indeed been here before. An old ice cream shop he used to frequent as a kid still stood at the end of the strip, but the other stores were new, unrecognizable.

Bill and the other agents climbed out of their cars. Bill opened the back door for Eddie.

"Right this way, Eddie." He spoke.

They walked Eddie to the middle section of the mall, where a door displayed an "FBI" sign with a star logo. *Strange,* Eddie thought, *that they don't have their own building.*

"I haven't been here in a very long time." Eddie commented. "The only thing I remember is that old ice cream shop. I would never have guessed your office would be over here."

The agents merely glanced at him from the corners of their eyes, saying nothing, and led him through the door. They passed a counter on one side and a bench on the other, then proceeded down a corridor to a door at the very end. They walked through it, only to find themselves outside again—but it was dark. No parking lot, no buildings, just a dirt road, a wooden fence, and surrounding trees and brush, as if it were nighttime. He saw other agents leading people to another area. Bill and his men took Eddie in the same direction, across the road and along a narrow trail. A chain-link fence lined one side of the trail; the other sloped sharply down to a lake. The group reached the other side. The agents then made them sit on a small retaining wall. Metal bars were behind them, and each person was cuffed to a bar before the agents left.

The group murmured amongst themselves, wondering what was happening and why this place felt like night when it was clearly midday outside the building. Suddenly, a blood-curdling scream tore through the air, but it vanished as quickly as it came. For a few moments, the group sat in silence, a cold shiver crawling down their spines. An agent came down the path, uncuffed a man, and led him away. The remaining group members were able to slide down the metal rail, taking the spot where the man had just been sitting. Eddie's new vantage point offered a better view across the lake and through some brush, allowing him to make out part of a street with a light post. He saw people walking around and agents positioned near them. He then saw a group hauling something on what looked like a big square gurney, four people, one at each corner. He couldn't quite tell what they were carrying.

"Hey, what are they carrying?" He asked the others.

The group looked, only to be horrified by

what they saw: two groups carrying piles of dead bodies down the street before disappearing. Mortified, they all panicked, wondering if that would be their fate later.

Another agent came to get another person, but Eddie spoke up. "Excuse me, Sir!"

"What is it?" The agent asked.

"Well, I need to use the restroom. I haven't gone since, well, before you guys picked me up this morning."

"Well, I guess it couldn't hurt to let you go use the restroom really quickly. I'll let you go, but you must come right back. Not like there's anywhere you can run to in here."

He un-cuffed Eddie and said, "Okay, walk down this path on your right, you'll see the restrooms."

"Yeah, I saw them on the way in, I know where they are, thanks!" Eddie said.

Eddie started down the path. The path was narrow, barely enough for one person, two only if they squeezed close. Ahead, he saw a figure walking briskly towards him, showing no signs of slowing down. As the figure nears, he saw it was a woman, seemingly in a trance. She came almost to him, and Eddie had to jump to the side, her leg brushing his shin.

"HEY! WATCH OUT!" Eddie yelled.

But she just kept going in full stride. *What the hell is going on here?* He thought.

He used the restroom, then walked back to the group. An agent waited for him there. The other agent picked up another person, but this time it was different: he led the man to the ledge and told him to jump. The man looked down at the dark water below, then back at the agent, who nudged him with a slight push. The man looked down again and jumped. A moment later, they heard the crashing sound of him hitting the water.

One by one, they were all made to jump down to the lake below. Eddie's turn was next. He stood on the edge, looking down, but it was so dark he could barely see the water, nor could he see the people who had jumped before him. Eddie leaped off the edge, free-falling for a few moments until he hit the water with tremendous force.

Eddie woke up, lying on the floor, having just rolled off the bed. His side and arm ached from the landing. Caroline woke up and looked down at him.

"Honey, you, okay? How in the world did you fall off the bed?"

"Yeah, I'm fine, sore, but I'm fine. That's the first time that's happened to me."

"What happened?"

"I had a crazy dream. I had to jump off this ledge, into a lake from high up. When I hit the water, that's when I landed on the floor." He explained.

"Wow! What is with you and your dreams?" She said. "You've had some weird dreams ever since we moved here. Is it the house?"

"I don't know what's with my dreams either. And no, I don't think anything is wrong with the house; it's just old." He replied.

"Well, maybe you've overworked yourself, or maybe something has happened to you that you didn't think about since we moved here?" She pondered.

"I don't think so. I don't remember anything happening to me since we've been here."

"Well, we'd better get back to sleep. We both might have a long day tomorrow." He suggested.

She agreed, and the light went out.

Two rooms down, Joey was awake. He had seen the figure of the man sitting in the chair across his room just moments before he heard a thud from his parents' bedroom. He'd vaguely heard what happened, but he decided to stay in bed, unsure where the man had gone. He slowly drifted back to sleep.

In the morning, they all woke up. Joey ran down the stairs as he always did, his mom and dad right behind him. They had their breakfast and got ready for their day. Eddie took the day off from work to handle things around the house. Joey ran out of the house and kissed his mom goodbye before she drove off for work. He did his chores while Eddie worked on the woodshed, which was almost done and would likely be finished by midday. While Eddie was on one side of the house, Joey was on the other, doing his chores. As he fed the chickens, he heard something coming from the direction of the house. He looked over but saw nothing. He went back to throwing feed and heard it again. This time, he looked at the house and saw a white silhouette of a person in a window at the end of the hall. As he watched, the figure moved out of view. Goosebumps rose on Joey's arms, and this time, he decided to head inside to investigate. He entered through the back door and went upstairs to the window where he had just seen the figure, but no one was there. He checked the rooms—nothing. He headed back downstairs and outside again to finish feeding the chickens.

Meanwhile, back with Eddie, he had just finished the shed and called out for Joey.

"JOEY! COME ON OVER HERE!" Eddie yelled.

Joey came running up seconds later.

"Yes, Dad? What did you need?"

"Help me move the firewood into the shed. Just got the shed done. What do you think, son?" Eddie asked.

"Sure, Dad, I can help you. And it looks good. When are you working on this creepy old house?"

Eddie pondered what his son had just said. "Well, son, that's the next project. And it's not creepy; it's just rustic and old. I think I'll start working on the porch next."

Eddie started walking towards the house. He stood in front of it, studying it. Joey watched his dad looking over the front of the house before he moved on.

Evening came, and Caroline pulled up. Joey ran out of the house to greet her while Eddie stood in the doorway with a smile.

"Hi, Mom!"

"Hello, little Bear! How's your day?" She spoke. While Joey talked to her, she looked up at Eddie, waved, and winked.

"It was a good day, Mom! Dad finished the woodshed, and then Dad and I loaded all the wood into it. Dad says he wants to start working on the porch now." Joey reported.

"Oh, is that so? You're going to help him, right?"

"Yes, Mom, of course I'll help him."

They both walked up to the door. Joey headed inside, and Caroline gave Eddie a hug and a kiss before entering.

Caroline started making dinner. Eddie went out to put away tools and get his gear ready for the next day's work. Tomorrow was his last day off, and he wanted to do as much as he could to the house. Joey would most likely go with his mom to work at the store and perhaps play with his friends in town.

Caroline called to Joey, "Joey, go up and wash up for dinner."

"Okay, Mom."

He ran up the stairs. Halfway up, he ran into an ice-cold spot. A feeling of self-doubt washed over him, as if by chance, he shouldn't proceed any further up the stairs. He decided to take it slow, carefully walking the remaining way up the steps as the icy spot dissipated. He went into the bathroom and washed his hands. He heard something behind him, like footsteps, but saw nothing in the mirror.

He called out, "Dad?"

"Yes?" His dad replied from just down the hall.

"Oh, nothing, I just heard you walking past, but I didn't see you go by." He stated.

"Oh, okay, son."

They both headed down to the dinner table together.

"Did you want to go with me to the store tomorrow?" Caroline asked Joey.

Joey pondered the idea. It had been a while since he was in town, and the house had been creepier than normal. He decided, "Yes, Mom, I'll go with you. Do you mind if I go see my friends too?"

"Why, sure, just help me out when we get there, and after lunch, you can go play with your friends."

They were all seated around the table, eating supper. They heard something upstairs, a heavy thud, nothing more. They all looked up at the ceiling, then at each other, asking, "What was that?"

Eddie got up from the table. "I'll go up and see what that was. Something must have just fallen."

He headed up the stairs. Caroline and

Joey, both heard him moving up there and then above them and then walking back down into the kitchen.

"What was it, honey?" Caroline asked.

"I don't know, honestly. Nothing was on the floor anywhere; everything seemed to be where it should be. Maybe it's just the house settling?" Eddie pondered before going back to eating.

"Oh yeah, maybe that's what it was. After all, it is an old house."

They went back to eating and talking about their day. Joey finished his plate and headed upstairs to get ready for bed. As he went up the stairs and to the bathroom, oddly enough, nothing happened to him this time. He found it odd but figured, *well, I still have until I get in bed, or maybe something will happen tonight,* he pondered. Shortly after he got upstairs, his parents came up to get ready for bed as well. They headed to their bedroom and changed.

Joey went to his room. It was a hot night. He opened the window and looked around outside before lying down. It was pitch black, only making out some nearby trees with the light coming from his bedroom. It was always the same, though—quiet as can be.

Still no wind, no crickets chirping. As always, he didn't pay any attention to it. He turned back, turned off the light, and went to sleep.

Caroline, Eddie, and Joey were fast asleep. But then, one by one, they were awoken by the sounds of footsteps walking up and down the hallway. Thump, thump, thump, and back the other way. Joey was the first to hear it. He looked at the clock. It was about 1:30 AM. He got up and walked over to his door. He opened the door and found no one there. Whoever was walking around stopped right when his door opened, and it was quiet again. He looked around, finding no one. He went back to bed and back to sleep. Moments later, the footsteps returned. This time, Caroline and Eddie heard them. Eddie got up and went to open the door. He opened it, and the sound went away. He even looked around, finding no one. Puzzled, he went back to bed.

"What was it? Was that Joey?" Caroline asked.

"I... don't know? It's not Joey; he is in his room laying down."

They went back to sleep, only to be woken up again. They went to the door and opened it, and nothing again.

Eddie called out, "HELLO?"

But no reply. He looked around the house and found nothing. He wandered back to bed, and they all went back to sleep.

Chapter Six:
The Walking Man
August 10, 1957

*T*he next morning, the house was quiet, but that same tension lingered. Joey still couldn't shake what he heard in the night. With fall settling in, the store had slowed down, as had the work at the ranch.

Their days had fallen into a quiet routine. At night, however, the footsteps in the hallway continued—soft and steady: *thump, thump, thump*—always stopping the moment someone stirred or opened a door. Even leaving the doors ajar didn't change anything; the moment they looked, the sound would stop. Joey still felt icy cold spots in the house, especially on the stairs and now in the hallway.

It was another night of the same unsettling pattern.

The next morning, a fresh blanket of snow covered the ground. Caroline was the first to step outside. As she made her way to the car, something caught her eye: footprints in the snow, circling the house. They trailed in both directions—around the front, and to both sides. An eerie chill ran up her spine. She turned back and called inside.

"Eddie! Come outside!"

"I'm coming!" He called, descending the stairs.

He stepped out the front door and saw her standing frozen near the car, her gaze fixed on the ground. "What is it, dear?"

"There are footsteps going around the house." She said, her voice low and uneasy.

Eddie looked down. Sure enough, the tracks going what seemed to be going to the back of the house on both sides. Concerned, he went back inside and grabbed the pistol he kept for safety.

"Stay here." He told her.

He walked the perimeter, following the steps. They didn't veer off in any direction— just a perfect circle. No trail in, no trail out. Just an endless loop. He met Caroline back at the front.

"Well? Was there anyone back there?"

He took off his hat and scratched his head. "No. No one. The tracks just go around. That's it."

"In a full circle?"

"Yep. No starting point. No ending point.

Unless someone was dropped off by a helicopter and then picked up again, I have no clue how."

She folded her arms tightly across her chest. "So, what do we do?"

"I don't know. Not much we can do right now, I guess. Let's just see if it happens again."

They both looked down at the tracks, the fresh snow making them stark and strange. Eddie kissed her goodbye, and Caroline headed off to work.

Inside, Eddie called upstairs. "Joey, are you ready to work?"

"Yeah, Dad, I'll be right down!"

Joey began walking down the hallway when a sudden burst of fast, stomping footsteps thundered behind him. He jumped aside in panic and spun around—no one was there. Just still air and a rush of wind.

"Dad?" He called softly.

"DAD?" Louder now.

"DAD!!" He screamed, fear taking over.

Eddie rushed to the stairs. "What is it, son?"

Joey sprinted into his father's arms.

"Something just ran at me in the hallway—right behind me. I jumped, turned around, and no one was there!"

Eddie held him tight. "It's okay. Nothing here is going to hurt you."

He looked up the stairs, seeing nothing, but his instincts said otherwise.

"Tell you what." Eddie said, pulling back. "Let's go get Mom and have breakfast together. Does that sound good?"

Joey nodded. Eddie guided him out to the truck. Joey climbed in without a word and stared at the floor the whole ride into town.

They pulled into the store.

"Wait here, son. I'll get your mom."

Inside, Eddie found Caroline stocking a shelf. "Hey, honey? I need to talk. Can we step outside for a minute?"

"Sure, what's going on?"

"It's Joey." He began. "After you left, something happened. I don't know what exactly, but it scared him terribly. I think there's more going on than he's told us. Think you can step away from the store for a bit?"

She paused, thinking. "It's probably going to be slow with the snow anyway. I'll just close up shop and reopen later."

She wrote a quick note for the door,

grabbed her coat, and joined Eddie in the truck. They drove in silence to their favorite breakfast spot.

The waitress greeted them with a smile. "Your usual table?"

"Actually, can we get that corner one today?" Eddie asked.

"Of course, go right ahead."

They sat—Joey between them, still quiet. After ordering, Eddie leaned in.
"Joey, tell your mom what happened."

Joey recounted everything. Caroline listened intently, eyes wide as he described the hallway incident, the sensation of being watched while he slept, the figure in the chair.

"Oh my!" Caroline stammered.
"Son" She said gently, "Is there anything else you haven't told us?"

Joey nodded. "Sometimes I wake up and... it's like something's there, just out of sight."

She took his hand. "Joey, we believe you. Your dad and I both do."

Joey looked up, relief washing over his face. "Really?"

"Yes." Eddie said firmly. "We do."

Caroline turned to Eddie. "What do we do now?"

"I think you and Joey should stay at the hotel for a few days. We'll just tell people something happened at the house—plumbing, electrical, whatever. I'll stay at the house and see what I can find out."

"Are you sure that's a good idea?"

"Yeah. Outside of the footsteps, nothing's happened to me."

"Okay. But promise you'll come get us if anything changes."

"Promise."

They finished their meal. Eddie dropped Caroline back at the store and took Joey to school, walking him to the door.

"After school, Mom will pick you up. You can pack a bag and head to the hotel. Sounds good?"

Joey nodded. "Thanks, Dad. Love you."

"Love you too. Keep this between us, okay?"

Back home, Eddie sat in the truck for a long minute, staring at the house. Finally, he stepped out and went inside. The house was quiet. Still. He climbed the stairs, checking the hallway. Nothing looked out of place. He stomped around in a few spots on the floor.

Nothing strange. Eventually, he headed out to his shop to work on the porch beams.

Hours later, Caroline tapped him on the arm. He jumped.

"Whoa! You scared the hell out of me!"

"Sorry! So? Did anything happen while we were gone?"

Eddie shook his head. "Nothing. I checked everything upstairs, stomped around... but I still think Joey really did experience something. I've been outside since."

"Still want us to stay at the hotel?"

"I do. I'm going to investigate the history of the house. I'll also get more done while it's quiet."

She nodded. They hugged, Eddie kissing them both goodbyes.

Back inside, Eddie reached for the light switch at the end of the hallway and got zapped. He cursed, flipped it again—another zap. He went down, shutting off the breaker, and fetched a new switch from the shop. He took the old one out of the wall. The switch had already begun to melt from faulty wiring. *"This could've burned the whole place down."* He muttered, replacing it carefully.

Later, he called Caroline. Joey was

doing well, and nothing odd had happened since they left the house. That night, Eddie left his door open, as always. But for the first time in months, he slept through the night.

The next morning, he met Caroline at the store.

"Morning, handsome! How was the night?"

"Uneventful. I replaced that light switch at the top of the stairs—it was melting down. We could've had a fire. Other than that, I slept all night. First time in forever."

"We did too." Caroline said. "Not a single thing happened."

Three days passed without an incident. They decided it was safe to return.

That night, Joey climbed the stairs, brushed his teeth, and peeked around before going to bed. Caroline and Eddie followed soon after. They all slept soundly.

At breakfast the next morning, Joey spoke up. "Mom? Dad? Have either of you heard or seen anything?"

They exchanged glances.

"No." Caroline said. "Nothing."

Eddie shook his head. "Me neither... You know, after I replaced that switch, the sounds stopped. Makes me wonder..."

He trailed off in thought, then said, "Maybe we had a guardian ghost."

Joey spoke up. "Yeah! I called him The Walking Man."

They sat in quiet reflection...

Chapter Seven:
Policy's Truth
December 13, 1957

*I*t was a cold, dark night, the air unnervingly still. A thunderous crash of metal on concrete snapped Eddie awake. Curled beneath a ragged sleeping bag, his head exposed to the brisk night air, he lay under a bridge, tucked inside one of the old concrete tubes meant as a tornado shelters, looking homeless and worn. He could see his breath in the single remaining headlight of a car, almost torn in half, its wreckage against the bridge support column stark in the dead of night. Shocked, he started to get up, but then, with a jolt, he truly awoke. It had all been a bad dream. After some time, the lingering terror faded, and he drifted back to sleep.

The next morning, the family rose and went their separate ways. Joey was off to school, Caroline to the store, and Eddie to the ranch.

Eddie had a busy day at the ranch, but after a few hours, he headed into town for some supplies. He decided to stop in at the store to see his wife.

"Hey, sweetheart, how's your day?"

Eddie asked, walking through the store, seeing her on the other side, meticulously stocking shelves.

"You know, for a Friday in the midst of winter, it's been really busy. Sales are up today, so I'm happy." She replied. "I'll be right with you in just one minute." She called out to a waiting customer.

"Yeah, I can tell." He said, looking around. "Same here. I just wanted to see you and check in to see how you're doing. I'm off to the next stop to pick up some stuff for the ranch." He turned to walk out the door. "Love you, honey, see you tonight!" He told her.

She smiled. "Love you too! Thanks for stopping in to see me." She turned and walked to the customer.

Eddie walked out the door and headed down the sidewalk towards his truck. He noticed a man approaching him, someone distinctly out of place, not from around here. Eddie looked closer, trying not to stare directly. The man was clearly a foreigner, perhaps from Asia, though Eddie couldn't pinpoint where from. He wore a black short-sleeved shirt with brown wool pants, a black and white neckerchief with red bands at both ends, and rubber sandals. He looked as if he had just emerged from the Amazon jungle. The man walked right up to Eddie, and as he passed, he looked directly into Eddie's eyes and said, "Ulineun dangsin-ui kkum-eseo dangsin-eul jab-eul geos-ibnida." Without breaking stride, the man continued walking away.

Eddie stared after him. "What did you say? I didn't understand you!" He called.

The man walked on, never stopping, and disappeared around a street corner. Eddie walked to where the man had turned. Peering around the corner, he found the man lying on the ground, a gunshot to his head and one to the chest. Eddie looked back at the street and yelled for help to the few people who were out; he kept shouting, "HELP, a man has been shot!"

As he turned back to offer aid, the man was no longer there.

Eddie, stunned, spun back to face the street. One man was coming to help, but Eddie didn't even see him. He just scanned back to where the man had just been, seeing nothing— no blood, no body, nothing. As he stood there, confused, the approaching man stopped him. "Where is he?" The man looked around, seeing no one.

"Ah... I... Don't know. He was right

there!" Eddie pointed as he spoke.

Eddie walked up to his truck; His hand clutched the door handle but couldn't bring himself to get in. *Who was that man?* He thought. Had he seen him before? He couldn't shake the man's face from his mind. He stood there, wondering what on earth the man had said to him before vanishing. It was snowing, and unnervingly quiet. After a while, he finally got in his truck, started it up, and continued with his day, the unsettling encounter replaying in his mind.

Back at work, Eddie found it hard to focus. All his thoughts revolved around that man, leading him into deeper reflections about past events. He wondered if he had indeed encountered this man before but simply didn't remember where. And the weirdest part, he thought, was the fact that the man had been lying there dead, dead in an alley just around the corner from his wife's store.

Suddenly, he started having intense flashes—vivid flashbacks of men screaming and explosions. So many flashes hit him that he lost his balance and fell off his chair to the floor. As quickly as the flashes came, they stopped the moment he hit the floor. He just sat there for a minute, dusted off his jeans, and picked himself up. Unsure what was happening to him, he called it a day, explaining to Vinnie that he didn't feel well and was going home, but would be back the next day.

At home, he couldn't make sense of what had transpired. So, he poured himself a tall shot of whiskey—his version of medicine—and went upstairs to lie down. He closed his eyes, and before long, he fell asleep.

Chapter Eight:
The Rude Awakening
November 7, 1958

*E*ddie jolted awake in the dead of night. No sound had roused him; no movement stirred the air—he simply awoke. As consciousness slowly seeped in, his eyes struggled to adjust to the oppressive darkness until a shape began to coalesce in the deepest corner of the room, just beyond his bedside table. A dark, hunched figure shifted, slowly detaching itself from the shadows.

Frozen, a primal terror seizing his limbs, Eddie could only watch. This was no dream. This was a nightmare given form, a vision out of fiction books or ancient biblical texts. The creature was impossibly thin, a skeletal silhouette of the darkest gray, almost black, its surface seemingly drinking what light there was in the room. Its eyes, twin points of piercing black and malevolent red, locked onto him with chilling intensity. Bony, elongated arms ended in sharp, pointed fingers that twitched, poised to strike.

With a speed that defied belief, the entity surged forward. With tremendous force, it slammed into Eddie's chest. The piercing fingers felt like burning talons entering his flesh. Violently shoved from his bed, he arced through the air before hitting the floor on the opposite side with a sickening thud.

A guttural gasp of pain escaped him as true consciousness snapped back. He lay sprawled on the cold floor, his chest aching with unbearable intensity. Lifting his shirt, he saw them: five raw, angry marks etched into his skin, mirroring the ghostly rake of those spectral fingers. Stunned, propped on one arm, he scanned the room. Caroline wasn't there. A small relief, perhaps, as she would have been pulled down with him. He remembered her being downstairs, engaged in some late-night tasks.

He heard her footsteps on the stairs, nearing the room. He scrambled up, still cradling his throbbing chest, meeting her at the doorway.

"What happened?" Caroline exclaimed, her voice thick with concern." It sounded like you fell off the bed! Like you were going to fall through the floor or something!"

"I... I had a dream." He began, his voice rough with lingering shock. "Or what I thought was a dream. This creature, this thing, was over by the bedside table. It came at me and shoved me completely off the bed." He lifted his shirt, exposing the vivid red welts.

Her eyes widened, her jaw dropping. "Oh my God, Eddie! Are... are you okay?" She stammered, her voice a hushed whisper of horror.

She reached out, her fingers softly tracing the marks, careful not to inflict more pain. Eddie had a high pain tolerance, but the sight alone suggested excruciating agony.

"Yeah, I'm okay." Wincing in pain. "It hurts like hell, but I'm okay. I just... I can't believe something like this happened to me."

He started to move past her, heading towards the stairs.

"Where are you going?" Turning to follow him.

"Well, since I was so rudely awakened, I might as well go down and get a drink." He replied, holding his chest and descending the stairs one careful step at a time, trying not to worsen the pain.

"Do we have any painkillers, by chance?"

"Yes." She called from behind him. "In the kitchen cabinet, top right, just before the sink."

She followed him down the stairs and

collapsed onto the couch, her gaze still fixed on him with a mixture of fear and disbelief.

Just a few feet away, Joey, roused by the loud thud and hushed voices, was already awake. He crept to his window, peering out into the impenetrable blackness of the night. The only light was the pale glow from his own room, illuminating the fall of snow near the pane. *Why is this happening to them*? he wondered. *Is this why I didn't like the house in the first place, or was it something else?* He considered speaking up sooner, sharing his unsettling feelings about the house when they first moved in. *But then, why would they listen to me? I'm just a kid.* He turned from the window, taking one last lingering glance at the swirling flakes, before retreating to the deceptive safety of his bed.

Morning arrived, gray and unwelcome. None of them had truly slept. Yet, the day demanded their attention. Caroline and Joey set off for town, Caroline dropping him off at school before heading to work.

"Mom, is Dad going to be okay? Are we going to be okay?" Joey's voice was filled with a tremor of fear.

"Your dad is a strong man, little Bear, so you don't need to worry about him any." She reassured him, her voice softer than usual. "As for us, we'll be fine. We three will figure this all out in time, I promise, okay?"

"Okay." He mumbled, turning his head to stare out the window, watching the world blur past.

Arriving at the school, she pulled up to the curb. "I love you, son! Have a good day!"

"Thanks, Mom! Love you too!" He replied, closing the door behind him. Caroline drove off, heading to work.

Meanwhile, Eddie had an easy day at work, starting at 5:30 AM and finishing around 2:00 PM. After picking up some supplies in town, he returned home and immediately began working on the house. He dashed inside only for a quick drink of water, then emerged, board by board, determined to fix what he could. By the time Caroline and Joey returned, he was exhausted but satisfied, ready for a break.

After a shower, he prepared dinner for the family, then settled into his easy chair. They gathered in the living room, watching a late-night show, each wondering what the coming hours might unfold.

One by one, they succumbed to sleep, the unspoken question of the night hanging heavy in the air. Yet, this night, unlike the last, nothing happened. It was one of the rare peaceful nights. When morning broke, Caroline, Eddie, and Joey shared breakfast. Eddie, fueled by a new resolve, returned to his work on the house. He was driven by a singular goal: to finish the renovations. Haunted or not, he decided, he would either make it livable or fix it up enough to sell it and move his family far away.

Eddie began working on the house siding. Joey came out to help when he could, and when he couldn't, he played nearby. Caroline joined them later, hanging laundry outside. Lunch brought a welcomed nice break: sandwiches, drinks, and conversations. Every now and then, Joey would glance up at the second-story window, a persistent feeling that someone was watching them. He never saw anything, no one looking back, but the sensation lingered.

As dusk began to settle, Caroline emerged to announce that dinner would be ready in about an hour, giving them ample time to finish and get cleaned up.

"DINNER'S SERVED!" She called up to them as they washed up. Both Eddie and Joey came down together, heading for the dinner table. Caroline had prepared a feast: pot roast with corn and mashed potatoes, and a scratch-made pie for dessert. As they ate, a series of soft pops and creaks echoed from upstairs. The distinct sound of footsteps, slow and deliberate, moving back and forth. They all stopped, forks halfway to their mouths, looking up at the ceiling, then at each other. Eddie's face hardened with a familiar grimace. "The Walking Man" was back.

He rose, tossing his napkin onto the table, and headed for the stairs. "I'll be right back." He stated.

Stepping through the kitchen doorway. He moved with a deliberate, unhurried pace. *Only one way in and one way out*, he thought, ascending the stairs to the landing. He surveyed the hallway; nothing. He walked down, checking each room methodically.

Joey and Caroline sat in strained silence at the table, listening as Eddie's footsteps ascended, then moved down the hall. They heard door after door creak open and shut— the main bedroom, the bathroom, then Joey's room. finding it empty. Yet, an odd compulsion drew him to the window. He scanned left and right, seeing nothing but the darkening landscape. Then, he looked down. In the damp snow below, clearly visible were muddy footprints in the snow. He peered closer, his breath catching on the windowpane. They were the same strange prints from months ago; those left in the snow.

A crack and a pop behind him startled him. He whipped around, focusing on the hallway, then back into the room. He stepped out and walked towards the bathroom. Inside, something was different. Muddy, bare footprints, fresh and undeniable, led directly to the mirror above the sink. They stopped there. No returning tracks. Something was still in the room, yet he saw nothing. He studied the prints again; they belonged to no animal or human he had ever seen. Puzzled, he slowly stood upright. He stared at the mirror, seeing only his own reflection, then glanced down at the prints behind him, then back at his reflection. He opened the medicine cabinet, finding nothing unusual. He closed it, turned, and started to walk out. But as he looked down, the prints were gone. Vanished. He stopped, looked back, then down at where he stood—nothing.

Stunned and profoundly confused, he descended the stairs, heading for the front door.

"Eddie, what happened? Did you find

anything?" Caroline asked, rising from the table, but he offered no reply as he walked straight out the door. She rushed after him, telling Joey to stay put.

Eddie walked around to the side of the house where he'd seen the tracks. The muddy prints in the snow were now smooth, flat, and trackless. He stood there, oblivious to Caroline calling his name, a profound chill seeping into his bones. He turned, looking up at Joey's window. And then, a shock. Standing in the frame, looking down at him, was what appeared to be a heavily bearded man in a dark brown, wide-brimmed hat. Just as quickly as Eddie registered the sight, the man vanished, dissolving into what could only be described as wisps of smoke. Then, nothing.

Eddie sprinted back inside, passing Caroline at the door.

"Someone was just in his room!" He exclaimed, tearing up the stairs. He burst into Joey's room, finding it empty, just as before. He checked the bathroom; nothing. He walked back to his son's room; Caroline went up the stairs, meeting him there. Eddie walked to the window, looking down at the ground, finding only his own footprints in the snow. He turned and looked at her, and the look in his eyes told her everything. Something profound and terrifying had just occurred. Shaking his head, Eddie walked to the door, leading her out and closing the door softly behind them.

Downstairs, they walked in silence. Their hunger gone, they returned to the kitchen, intending to finish their meal. But Joey wasn't there. They exchanged a bewildered glance.

"Where did he go?" Caroline whispered.

"I don't know, he was just here. We told him to stay here!" His voice strained.

Caroline frantically scanned the living room, thinking he might be hiding. Eddie rushed back outside, checking around the house, the workshop, and the woodshed. No sign of him. He returned inside to find Caroline standing in the living room, her face pale.

"Did you find him?" She asked, though the answer was already etched in the fear in his eyes. He knew what he had to say wouldn't make it any better. With a heavy sigh, he uttered the single, devastating word: "No."

Tears welled in her eyes. "He has to be here somewhere. We weren't gone more than five minutes."

They split up, widening their search,

their desperate calls echoing through the
suddenly too-silent house.

Chapter Nine:
Down by the River
November 8, 1958

*J*oey hung suspended, pinned to the kitchen ceiling, a silent scream trapped in his throat. From his terrifying perch, he watched in horror as his mother moved beneath him, her cries echoing through the house, calling his name repeatedly, but receiving no reply. He thrashed, he kicked, he strained against the unseen force that held him, but its grip was unyielding. He heard her frantic footsteps retreating to the living room, then the hushed, desperate voices of his mom and dad discussing him. Powerless, he listened as their footsteps faded, their search continuing, moving further away. A wave of darkness consumed him, and he blacked out.

"Where is he, Eddie? It's dark out and snowing! He's not inside, I've looked everywhere! Did you see any tracks? Anything?" Caroline pleaded, her voice edged with panic.

"No... I... I didn't find him, or any tracks either!" Eddie replied, his voice heavy with dread. "Did you check the closets? The bathroom? The pantry?"

"Yes! Everywhere! He's just... gone!" She cried. "What are we going to do? It's almost nine o'clock. Should we call the police?"

"I don't know. I guess... I guess I'll call the Sheriff." He mumbled, already reaching for the phone.

He waited as the line connected. "Hello? Yes... my son is missing. We've looked everywhere. My wife checked the house twice, and I've gone over the grounds and outbuildings twice as well. Yeah, it's snowing here. No, I didn't see any tracks in the snow either."

He paused, rubbing his forehead. "Wait—before all this, we were sitting at the table and heard something upstairs. I went to check, didn't see anything, but when I looked out my son's window, I saw tracks in the mud. My wife came up just as I was heading out to follow them, but by then... the prints were gone."

Another pause. "Okay... how long? Thirty to forty-five minutes? Got it. My wife, Caroline, will be here to meet you. I'm going to head down the road and see if I can find him. I'll meet you back here in an hour. Thanks, Sheriff."

Eddie hung up the phone.

Walking to Caroline, who was openly weeping, and pulled her into a tight embrace.

"We will find him!" He promised, his voice firmer than he felt. He pulled on his coat and walked out the door, into the swirling snow.

Eddie drove slowly down the winding road towards town, his eyes scanning every shadowed ditch and snow-laden tree, desperately hoping to glimpse his son. On a narrow, straight stretch of road, he sped up, driven by urgency. Suddenly, the car hit a patch of black ice. He wrestled with the wheel, fighting for control, the bridge ahead looming. He managed to straighten the car just barely, but it was too late. The vehicle veered sharply off the road, catching the embankment, and launched into the air, flipping end over end. His car crashed down, roof-first, smashing through the brittle ice and into the half-frozen river below.

Submerged in the icy depths, Eddie was miraculously alive. Frigid water rushed in, filling the cab. He struggled desperately with his seatbelt, fumbling with the clasp until it finally gave way. With a surge of adrenaline, he kicked out, shattering out what remained of the windshield, and pulled himself free just moments before the truck plunged entirely beneath the surface, only its rear tires left exposed to the snowy air. He floated downstream for a short distance before his numb limbs found the strength to propel him towards the shoreline. He clawed at the tall, frosted weeds, dragging himself from the water.

Gasping for breath, he lay there, soaked and shivering, water still gurgling in his ears.

He shook his head violently to clear them. It was then that he heard it: a muffled, distant sound, like gunfire and screaming. His ears popped, and the sounds sharpened – three distinct bursts of gunshots, then the rat-a-tat of automatic fire, what was frozen land was now green. Tall grasses and trees followed by the terrified cries of men. Flashes of light, followed by loud booms, erupted around him. He instinctively flattened himself, seeking cover in the tangled weeds.

Then, silence. Absolute, chilling silence.

But then, he heard it. A faint cry, a child's cry, carried on the wind. It was distant, almost swallowed by the night, but he knew that sound. It was Joey. The cries grew a bit clearer, Joey's voice, small and desperate, calling for help.

Eddie scrambled to his feet, ignoring the biting cold and the pain, and began to run towards the sound. He slipped and slid in the snow, fighting to maintain his balance, terrified of falling back into the river. Finally, he saw him. Just on the other side of the bridge, near the icy water, Joey was huddled in a fetal position, shivering violently, sobbing.

"JOEY! I'M HERE! I'M COMING TO YOU! STAY THERE!" Eddie roared, his voice hoarse but filled with a desperate hope.

He reached Joey, pulling his son into his arms. Joey was icy cold, trembling uncontrollably. Eddie lifted him, and together, they began the painful journey back to the road. As they neared the ascent, Eddie heard the distinct hum of an approaching car. He looked over and saw them: the flashing red and blue lights, cutting through the snowy haze in the distance. The sheriff.

The patrol car pulled up, stopping directly in front of them. The Sheriff stepped out, peering through the headlights' glare. "Eddie, is that you?"

"Yes!" Eddie yelled back, pulling Joey closer. "I have Joey! We both need help!"

The Sheriff quickly helped them both into the warmth of the car.

"Sheriff, take us home!" Eddie urged, his teeth chattering. "It's too far to go to the hospital. We need to get warm. Joey's starting to turn blue."

With lights blazing, the Sheriff accelerated, heading back towards Eddie's home.

Back at the house, Caroline saw the approaching lights and raced inside, waiting anxiously at the door. As the Sheriff pulled up, she rushed out to meet him. To her surprise, the two back doors of the patrol car opened. She saw a tall man rise from one side, and then a small figure emerged from the other. As the car lights dimmed, she realized it was Eddie and Joey.

She sprinted towards Joey.

"We need to get him inside quickly!" Eddie called out. "He's freezing!"

They all rushed inside, helping Joey to the fireplace, wrapping him in every blanket they could find. Eddie ran upstairs to change out of his soaking, half-frozen clothes. Once dressed, he headed back down, finding the Sheriff already questioning Joey. The Sheriff paused when he saw Eddie approaching.

"So, Eddie, you said you lost control by the bridge and crashed into the river, correct?"

"You crashed your truck!" Caroline exclaimed, her eyes wide with shock. "What? Are you okay?"

Eddie, looking at both, replied, "Yes, I'm okay, and yes, I crashed. I lost control and ended up upside down in the river. But thank God, had I not, I don't think I would have known he was down there."

"So, Joey?" The Sheriff interjected, turning back to the boy. "You were saying you were taken there by something, then you woke up by the river?"

Joey, shivering less but still trembling, looked at his mom and dad, then back at the Sheriff.

"Yes, I remember being here. I saw them looking around for me, but something had me... I... I couldn't... call out to them!" Joey choked out, tears welling in his eyes.

"So, you both were looking for him before he was taken, but you didn't see him?" The Sheriff clarified.

Both Caroline and Eddie affirmed simultaneously.

She continued, her voice pleading. "Sheriff, we looked everywhere for him. We never saw him leave. Maybe you should look around, see if you find anything out of the norm. If someone took him like he says, maybe you can find out who?"

The Sheriff nodded, asking if he could look around freely. They agreed, and he stepped back out into the snowy night.

"Sheriff! Thanks for coming!" Eddie called out. "I don't know what we would have done if you hadn't found us."

The Sheriff gave a curt nod and headed out to search the house and the surrounding property.

Once the Sheriff was out of earshot, Eddie turned to Joey. "Joey, what happened, son?"

Joey replied. "I couldn't say anything with the cop here; he wouldn't believe me!"

"What is it, Joey?" Caroline urged, her voice soft but firm.

Joey recounted the terrifying evening: being held to the ceiling, watching them search below, unable to make a sound. Then, the sudden, jarring awakening in the freezing cold by the river. He described hearing a car approaching, then a crash downriver, followed by a chilling silence. Later, the muffled sounds of someone coughing and grunting. Only then did he manage to cry out for help. That's when he heard someone coming towards him.

"It was you, Dad!" Joey sobbed, tears streaming down his face. Moments later, the Sheriff re-entered the house, walking directly to them.

He addressed them all. "Eddie, family, I saw nothing out of place. No other tracks besides the shoes you both are wearing. Son, was it only you down by the river where you woke up?"

Joey replied, "Yes."

"Okay. I think I'll head back down the road. I'll set up a marker for your truck so we can find it easier for the morning tow truck. I'll do some looking around where you found Joey at; there has to be something around there, perhaps." The Sheriff spoke as he walked towards the door. "I'll be back shortly. Joey, are you okay? Do you think he or you, Eddie, are needing to go to the hospital?"

Eddie thought for a minute before replying, "I think we're okay for now, but if we need to go, we'll take the car. I think you should take a look around first. If we decide to go, we'll stop by on the way to talk to you."

"Okay, family, be safe. I'll stop back by... say, in about an hour from now, as long as this storm holds up."

"Sounds good, Sheriff, thanks again for

saving us!" Eddie called back.

They all stood by the fireplace, warming themselves from the night's nightmares. Joey and Eddie, both wrapped in blankets, shared silence, knowing looks that spoke volumes. Before they knew it, a knock echoed at the door. Startled, they all jumped.

"Yes? Enter!" Eddie called out.

"Hey, all!" The Sheriff announced as he walked in. "Just wanted to let you know I got your truck marked. I also saw nothing out there. So, that said, I don't understand how Joey got there." He wiped the brim of his hat, smearing the water onto his jeans. "I saw your tracks, Eddie, going from the shore to Joey and then the tracks to the road where I found you two. So, I don't really understand what happened. But I'll keep my eye out for anything unusual around here and in town. How are you two doing?"

"Thanks, Sheriff, for everything!" Eddie stated. "I don't know what happened either. We're doing better and about thawed out, finally. Thanks for coming back to check on us."

"You're welcome, all. Have a good night, call me if you need anything!" He said while glancing around looking to the top of the stairs pausing shortly, as he walked to the door.

Caroline walked him out. "Thanks again!" She whispered as the door closed.

She stood there, watching the headlights disappear into the darkness.

Eddie pushed himself up, unsteady on his feet. He looked at his family, asking the question.

"Should we just head to bed? Joey, you want to sleep in our room?"

Joey hesitated. "Yeah, I'll sleep in your room." He said, voice trembling slightly.

"Okay, baby bear, go upstairs and get ready. We'll be right up in a few." Caroline told him gently.

Joey walked wearily up the stairs. They heard water running once he reached the bathroom.

"Eddie! What are we going to do?" Caroline whispered, her voice cracking.

"Right now? Try to sleep. We'll figure this all out in the morning." He said, taking a heavy breath.

They all headed to bed for the remainder of the night.

Chapter Ten:
The Burn
November 14, 1958

Weather-related issues had kept Eddie's truck submerged for days but today was finally the day. He stood by the riverbank, the biting November wind whipping at his coat, his gaze fixed on the icy water. A few men worked with practiced efficiency, rigging the submerged vehicle, preparing to winch it from the frigid depths. The tow truck roared to life, its diesel engine a harsh counterpoint to the desolate, snow-covered landscape. The sounds of straining pulleys and groaning cables echoed, taut with effort.

Suddenly, a profound dizziness washed over Eddie. He swayed, his hands instinctively clenching, and he fought to steady himself. The familiar winter scene around him—the frosted trees, the gleaming ice, the distant, stark hills— blurred, then shattered. In its place, an alien, vibrant world erupted. Tall, impossibly green grasses rose around him, dense trees and thick, oppressive shrubs creating a sweltering jungle. Men, clad in unfamiliar fatigues, sprinted past, their rifles clutched in their hands. Explosions erupted, first a distant boom, then terrifyingly close beside him, sending plumes of flames roaring into the humid air. Screams—horrific, agonizing screams—tore through the jungle from every direction. Figures, consumed by fire, ran blindly, their cries choked by smoke, before collapsing to the ground.

"MOVE IT, MOVE IT!" A voice bellowed, hoarse with urgency, cutting through the inferno. Eddie had no idea who these people were or where he was. The frantic call came again, closer this time, searing into his terror.

"HEY, YOU! YOU NEED TO MOVE!"

The tow truck driver's voice, sharp and insistent, pierced the hallucinatory vision. Eddie gasped, jolting back to reality, his hands flying to his face, wiping at nothing. He stumbled, nearly falling, but the driver's strong arms caught him.

"Eddie, hey, Eddie? You with me?" The driver asked, concern deeply etched on his face.

"Whoa! Oh my God!" Eddie stammered, his heart hammering against his ribs. He shook his head, trying to clear the lingering images. "Um... wow... I don't know what happened." He decided against disclosing the vivid, terrifying vision. "*He'll think I'm crazy!*" He thought, the thought cold and sharp amidst the fading heat of the hallucination.

Gathering his thoughts, Eddie looked up. His truck was already being lifted from the water, dripping mud and icy spray. He realized he was standing directly in the way. The driver, still casting a concerned glance his way, moved off to help his crew. Eddie and the driver's assistant stepped aside, watching as the mangled vehicle was slowly hauled up to the road, destined for the junkyard. Eddie remained, detached, his mind replaying the flashes of fire and green, the terrifying screams. He felt disoriented, adrift.

"Get moving! Move it! Move it!"

He heard the words echo over his shoulder, the same frantic urgency as in his vision.

"Huh? What?" Eddie mumbled, still lost in thought.

"Sir? We're done here!" The driver said, tapping Eddie on the shoulder.

Eddie realized he was kneeling on the ground, oblivious. He looked back at the driver. "Huh... What... oh, okay... thank you."

He slowly rose, his gaze drawn to his truck, now loaded and ready to go. He tipped the driver some cash, his movements stiff, before they drove off. Eddie walked to Caroline's car, taking one last look at the dark, swirling river, then got in. He sat for a moment, the engine idling, before turning the wheel. A perfect three-point turn, and then, home.

He arrived home ten minutes later. Walking up the porch steps, he opened the door and stepped inside.

"Hi, handsome!" Caroline said, her voice soft, knowing what he had just witnessed from his truck being hauled out of the river.

"Hi, my love!" His voice was flat, a distant look in his eyes.

"Honey?" Seeing the troubled expression on his face. "Did everything go smoothly?"

"Well, yes, but not without a hitch." The memory of the vision still vivid.

"What do you mean? What happened?" Sensing his unease.

"Well... they got the truck out easily enough... but, I had this—this episode."

He began describing the details, the vividness of the jungle, the running men, the explosions, and the horrific screams.

"Um... what does this mean, Eddie? Where do you think this is coming from? Is it this house, do you think?" A flicker of fear in her eyes.

"I... honestly, don't know." He admitted, looking around their home. "Maybe it's the house? Maybe it's me? I really don't know at this point. I mean, what about Joey? All the things that have happened to him? Maybe it's this house." He paused, the silence heavy in the room. "I think it's time." He finally said, his voice quiet but firm.

"Time for what?" She pondered, her brow furrowed.

"I... I think it's time to... go see our Pastor. I think we should go to our church... Hopewell in Edmond and see Pastor Hendrix. Maybe he can bless the house. Maybe he can help us all or at least know someone within the church that can?" He suggested, a glimmer of hope in his eyes.

"Well, I think it's worth a try. Let's go in the morning. We can take Joey with us and go for breakfast before our meeting." She said, a sense of resolve entering her voice.

Eddie walked to the phone, picked it up, and dialed. She stood nearby, close enough to overhear the conversation.

"Hello? ... Pastor Hendrix? Yes, Hi! It's Eddie Matters... Us? Well, that's why we're calling. So, we could be better... Yes, we would like to meet with you tomorrow morning if you have time? Oh… 9:00 AM." He looked at Caroline, who nodded her agreement. "Yes, yes, that works for us. Oh, yes, just us three: Caroline, Joey, and I. Ah, okay. Thanks, Pastor! We will see you tomorrow. Thanks, okay, bye." He hung up the phone. He looked at her. "Since the church is between here and Oklahoma City, I think we should stay at that old hotel we like."

"That sounds good to me, honey. JOEY! Pack a bag! We're going somewhere for the night!" She called out to Joey, who was doing some chores outside.

"OK, MOM! I'LL BE RIGHT IN!" Joey called back.

"So, it's almost 4:00 PM." Eddie stated. "Let's get the car packed soon and get moving. We don't want to be too late."

They all packed up, then headed out to the car. It was a freezing cold evening as they loaded their belongings, but the weather was clear enough for driving. They got in the car and headed down the road. The road so far wasn't too bad, just a few icy spots here and there. As they approached the bridge where Eddie had flipped his truck weeks before, and where he'd found Joey on the other side, neither he nor Caroline spoke or looked to either side. Joey, in the back, looked down, engrossed in a toy. Eddie was dead focused on the road ahead while he drove. Caroline sat in the passenger seat, reading the latest issue of Vogue magazine.

"Eddie?" She began, still looking at the magazine. "Do you think we should move? Maybe to a new state? Selling everything—the store, the house, the land? Move somewhere better?"

"I... well, I don't know? This is all I've ever known. This land, the people... it's safe here for Joey, excluding what's been happening to us. I... I don't know. I think we need to see what comes from the meeting with the Pastor and go from there. I've been working on the house when I can. I know this is what I wanted and how I've envisioned our house and us to be. But, at the same time, I must keep fixing it up so we can sell it if we must. You know, I'm about done. We still have some things to work on, but the house is coming along very well. I'm not even sure how I would be able to do all this myself if it weren't for the guys coming to help us when they can as well. Anyway... let's just see what happens after the blessing."

Eddie realized he had completely forgotten he was thinking about all the things that had happened at that bridge when they passed by.

In town, they made it to the diner. A quick and easy stop, and then back on the road they went, driving another hour to get to the hotel. They checked in, headed to their room, and by just after 6:00 PM, they were settling in. Now they only had a few more miles to go to get to the church in the morning. They unpacked their belongings and prepared for the remainder of the evening. Caroline turned the TV on. Eddie sat in the corner chair, watching Joey play with some toys while also unpacking. He watched as a toy Tyrannosaurus rex pulled a shirt from Joey's luggage and, with a roar, dropped it onto the bed. Eddie smiled, took off his hat, and turned his attention to his wife, giving her a reassuring smile. It was as if he knew that away from home, nothing would happen to them tonight. One by one, they took showers and got ready for bed. Two of them wondered what Pastor Hendrix would say to them tomorrow morning about all the things that had been happening.

"Caroline, Sugar." Eddie whispered to her as Joey was fast asleep. "Tomorrow, I'd like to go to Oklahoma City to see if I can find a new truck. I'll be needing something soon, so we can finish this house either way."

"I think that's a good idea!" She told him. "I don't see the Pastor being able to come right away to look at the house until the next day at best."

"Okay, honey, sounds good. Good night, love you." Kissing her good night.

They both quickly drifted off to a deep sleep.

Chapter Eleven:
The Ninth Night
August 14, 1959

Nine months had passed since Pastor
Hendrix first walked the halls of Eddie and
Caroline's home, uttering words they had never
heard in church before: "Ee Jip-Gwa ee sa-
ram-deul-eh-geh chook-bok-eul nae-ree-shi-
go, ee-got-eh een-neun mo-ak-han gi-oon-eun-
sa-ra-ji-geh ha-so-seo." He moved through
each room, his voice a steady chant, until a
profound stillness settled. The family thanked
him profusely, their gratitude deepening with
each passing week. From then on, they saw
him more often, attending church almost every
other Sunday.

It took time to adjust to the unsettling
silence that followed, a quiet that felt like both a
blessing and, strangely, a curse. The constant
anxiety of wondering if tonight would be "the
night" had faded, replaced by an unfamiliar
peace, a profound serenity. Joey still gazed out
his bedroom window, sometimes cracking it
open, listening to the perpetually dark, silent
nights. He watched the falling snow through
the remaining winter months, even building a
grand snowman right where his father had

seen those mysterious footprints so long ago, completely unaware of the spot's eerie past. Joey thrived that winter, even deciding to take the year-end test to advance a grade. He had the option to skip two grades but chose to stay with the friends he had made. He continued to help at the store and the ranch, taking on more responsibilities, whether fixing a tractor or taking inventory. He no longer felt watched, nor did he encounter the inexplicable cold spots in the house. Everything seemed perfect, especially since he had helped his dad finish the interior and exterior of their home just weeks before.

Eddie had completed all the work on the house and outbuildings. The cherry-inlaid door, the arched porch, the fresh paint—all were now weeks old, just as he had envisioned, with a few extra touches requested by Caroline. Her one small request had been for a new closet, cleverly tucked under the staircase. Life was unfolding beautifully for him and his family.

Work life flowed easily through the winter months. There were always enough hands to keep everything running smoothly, feeding livestock, shoveling snow, and plowing roads when needed. For the first time in a long time, everything just felt right. Eddie felt more at home here than anywhere in his past. Winter had been bitterly cold, but nothing compared to that one night on the river. He focused on the bright side: his family was safe, and most importantly, Joey was thriving.

Caroline couldn't have been better; she looked more alive than she had in years. The store thrived, even through the winter months. And Joey… she couldn't have been prouder of the young man he was becoming, helping at the shop, assisting his dad, and spending time with good friends. Who often came to hang around at the house. And the house itself— nice and tightly put together, just the way she liked it, now that Eddie and the men had finished their work. It looked magnificent, and she felt a surge of pride in the man she married; he truly was a great man.

Pastor Hendrix's work had undeniably succeeded. Whatever he did for them and the house, it worked. After church, he'd often stop them, checking if they'd experienced any more issues. Each time, they'd assure him, "No, Pastor, everything has been great. Thank you so much for everything." Eddie, grateful, would occasionally ask if the Pastor needed help at the church. When the Pastor had no specific tasks, Eddie would discreetly slip him some money. Pastor Hendrix, a truly great man, never once accepted payment for his extraordinary help. His only request was for them to contribute to the church, and they did. They helped plan and host events; Eddie even rebuilt sidewalks, crafted new pews, and constructed a new platform.

As the months gave way to August, the family seized a rare opportunity for a week-long vacation away from the store and ranch. During a slow period for both. They chose Colorado, a place they'd never visited but had heard so much about. In Denver, they drove to the Red Rocks Amphitheater, marveling at the nine-year-old structure, a new attraction just beginning to draw visitors from out of state.

They also explored Rocky Mountain National Park, gazing at the tall, majestic peaks. Joey was delighted, running and chasing birds and chipmunks in the open fields. Upon their return to the castle, which they called home in the foothills of Oklahoma, they found a lone figure standing in the driveway near the porch. Dressed all in black, the person's identity was unclear until they drew closer... It was Pastor Hendrix. In the ensuing conversation, Pastor Hendrix explained that he'd been checking on the

house every few days while they were away.
He'd even recited some blessings for the
house, one of which was:
"I jibi dangsin-deurui yeonghon-eul ppaeatgo,
amugeotdo namgiji ankireul."

Both Eddie and Caroline smiled, making
remarks like, "Oh, I don't know what you're
saying, but it sounds lovely!" Or "Wow, you
sure have a way with words!"

The Pastor would simply smile, nod, and
say, "Oh, these are words I learned in a
faraway land."

He'd also watered their plants and
ensured no one trespassed on their land.

It was August 14th, just over a week
since their return. It had been a quick
turnaround for both Caroline and Eddie as the
store and ranch geared up for the fall months.
Eddie ensured the crops were thriving, ready
for a timely harvest. Caroline worked diligently,
making sure the ranchers and townsfolk would
have what they needed when harvest season
arrived. Later that day, after long, tiring hours,
they all met back at their cozy home. They
settled in, turned on the radio to a popular
show of the time, and as dinnertime
approached, Caroline rose and headed to the
kitchen.

"What do you two want?" She asked. "We can have either hamburgers or chopped steak with gravy and mashed potatoes on the side?"

"Well, Joey—" BOOM! A deafening crash from upstairs cut Eddie off mid-sentence. He was about to suggest hamburgers for the night. Eddie sprang up and bolted for the stairs, shouting to Joey, "Stay there!"

Caroline emerged from the kitchen, her eyes fixed on the staircase, awaiting word from him.

"I think that it came from outside?" Eddie called down.

Caroline and Joey rushed out, Caroline telling Joey. "To stay on the porch for now."

Eddie followed right behind them. They began to walk around the house, soon discovering a large tree had fallen on top of it.

"Joey! It's okay, you can come here!" She called. He came running over to see what had happened. The tree rested precariously on the edge of the house, having only damaged the eaves.

"Well, I don't know about you two?" Eddie said, looking at Caroline and Joey. "But I'm wide awake now." He turned back towards the front door. "Honey, I think it's a burger kind of night, what do you say?"

"Sounds good to me!" She replied, following his footsteps.

Joey followed along, calling to his dad, "Dad! What now?"

"Well, I'm going to make a call." Eddie said, reaching for the phone. "Then we'll have our burgers, and after that, we'll take the tree off the roof before it gets dark. So, eat up quickly and be ready to work once you're done."

"Hey! Are you busy? Ah, perfect. Can you call two other guys to come up and help us remove a tree that landed on my roof? ... I can pay you your 'normal' wage! ... Alright, I'll see you in about forty minutes. Thanks! See you soon, bye." He hung up the phone.

"Joey, eat up quick! We need to be ready when the guys get here." He instructed.

They ate quickly and headed outside, setting up a ladder to the roof while Joey waited below. Eddie hauled a chainsaw up with him.

"Joey! Stand back!" He called down to his son. "I'm going to start cutting and throwing the branches down. Watch out for me. Once I cut one and throw it down, pick it up and take it to the road."

"Okay, got it!"

The two got to work, and Joey quickly found a rhythm. By the time he carried a load of branches to the road and returned, more were already waiting for him. He started with the first two, gathering more, deftly sneaking between drops. Then, a new sound reached them. Eddie paused, looking around for the source, and saw three men walking up, each with a chainsaw in hand.

Eddie shut down his saw. "Hey guys! Welcome to the disaster!" He called down with a half-hearted laugh. "Let me take these last few branches off, and I'll be down. Then we can plan how to get the main tree down."

"Sounds good, boss!" One man called up, while the other told Joey to help them out as well.

They geared up, started their saws, and began cutting away at the branches below, all careful to watch out for the limbs being cut above.

Eddie stopped, came down the ladder, and walked up to Joey, who was clearly struggling to keep up. "Joey, go take five... Get us some bottles of Hehi sodas."

"Okay." Joey replied, wiping sweat from his forehead.

He ran off to the kitchen, downed some water, took a minute to catch his breath, and then returned with the sodas for the four men.

"Thanks, Joey! You're the best!" They told him.

Each man took a bottle, slammed it down, and they were back to work. One man wrapped a rope around the fallen tree; the other secured the line to a nearby tree, then to the truck's back bumper.

One man started the truck, pulling the tree just enough to relieve some pressure and gain leverage off the house. This ensured that when they cut a section, it would fall to the ground below instead of into the house. They got the tree down, then began cutting it into manageable-sized pieces. Once they were finished, Eddie asked Joey to head inside and grab the payment. Joey returned with two cases of beer, then went back for a third—one for each man. Eddie thanked them as they climbed into their truck, fired it up, waved, and drove off down the road.

By 8:30 PM, the only thing left of the tree was a stump and a neat pile of wood.

"Joey, thanks for helping! You did a great job, son! Go up and take a shower and come back down, I'll have something for you."

Eddie told him.

Joey ran up and showered, then came down looking for his dad. He found him and his mom sitting at the kitchen table.

"Hey kiddo, come, have a seat!" They told him.

He sat down at the table; Eddie got up and went to the cupboards, getting a bowl. He set it down on the counter while reaching for the freezer door. He then got a container of ice cream and scooped out a big scoop into the bowl, handing it to Joey.

"Here you go, enjoy!" He said, smiling at him as he turned his head to look at Caroline, telling her and Joey, "I'm heading up now for a shower as well."

He turned and walked away, heading up the stairs. Starting the water, he climbed in, washing away the rush of the evening. The curtains ruffled gently with the spray of water running down the sides. Suddenly, the curtains ripped wide open, startling him. He looked around; no one was there. He closed the curtains again. Finishing his shower, he toweled off and headed for the door. Turning the corner, he jumped. Joey was standing there at the door's edge.

"Damn son, you scared the hell out of

me!" He said, laughing it off. "What ya doing, son?"

"Oh, nothing, I just want to ask you something... I heard the water stop, so I was just waiting here for you... Dad? Tomorrow? Can I sleep in and go see my friends afterwards?" He asked, the signs of exhaustion on his face.

"Well... huh... I think its Saturday tomorrow, so I think we can do better than that."

Joey, anticipating something grand, asked, "What's that, Dad?"

"I think you can sleep in for a while... but... no, you can't go hang out with your friends... I need you..." He said while Joey started to show signs of sadness. "I need you to do your chores first."

"Oh... okay, Dad..." Joey was sad but started to turn and go to his room when Eddie called back to him.

"Wait, son... I wasn't done yet!"

Joey turning back to face him. "I want you first, before your chores, to call your friends to come here to the house! So, by the time you finish up, your friends should be here. We will cook, have a party, and have a bonfire with the wood from the tree this evening! Your mom and I will have some people over as well! What do you say to that, kiddo?"

"Really, Dad?" He asked with excitement. "Um... does Mom know about this? Will she be okay with all the people here?"

The whole time, Eddie moved Joey in a half-circle so he wouldn't see his mom behind him.

"She does now! She's right behind you!"

Joey turned, seeing his mom and asking, "Mom? Really? Can we?"

"Yes, my little Bear, we can... It's overdue to have people over, and this is perfect timing. We can show everyone our nice house we have. And all the work you have been working on." She stated with a big smile on her face. "Now, son, get ready for bed and get some sleep." She said while looking at her husband with a spark in her eye.

"Okay, Mom... Thanks, Dad!" Joey ecstatically said.

They both said, "You're welcome." As they both went to get ready for bed. Sleep came fast for them all. It was a lot of work to bring down the tree so late at night after work. All was quiet until they were awoken up by creaking, and cracking noises coming from downstairs. Lights glowed from the living area, shining on the ceiling in the hallway outside their room.

"What in the world is going on?" Eddie nervously got out of bed and headed to the door.

Looking from over the edge of the railing to the stairs, dark purples, dark reds flickered from below him. Caroline and Joey, now behind him, looked onward. They made their way down the steps, each step seeming to take forever. With each step, a new noise came from the house. Crashing sounds, deep creaking and popping. They finally made their way to where the light was coming from: the new closet under the steps. They stood back as the door started to bend outwards more and more. You could see the light growing brighter and brighter from the top and bottom, to the point you could clearly see beneath and above the door. The inlays, which were still flat but had popped out from the door itself. The sounds were deafening. Eddie slowly walked to the door, fearing it might break in half. He knocked on the door. The sound stopped. The lights turned to a white glow; only a faint light was left from the door, allowing them to see clearly to the back of the closet.

"Hello...." Eddie called out to the closet.

Calling out after seeing bony, twig-like feet and legs slowly fall to the floor. They heard a dark groan coming from behind the door. A figure started to stand tall, hands high above it. Piercing eyes looked at them with cracks in its bone-like flesh. It clawed at the wall behind it and went up into the ceiling. Eddie looked on as it disappeared into the white paint above, leaving a trail of smoke in its wake. Eddie told the family to "Go outside now!" as a rumbling and awful noise filled every corner of the house. Grabbing jackets out of the closet on the way out. As they ran, passing the door frame, the noise was gone; it was eerily quiet now. They turned, looking at each other. Caroline was white as a ghost, and Joey in tears. They turned back, looking at the house. All the brush and trees were now bending towards the house. A frightening sight to behold. Eddie told them to get in the car. Eddie rushed back into the house, parts falling—not from the ceiling but rising from the floor towards the ceiling. He was quick, rushing to the keys on the counter. He ran out the door. The sound inside sounded so demonic, so dark, and just like last time. He exited the house, and it was quiet once more.

Eddie, throwing on an old green field parka, a jacket he hadn't worn in years. The family piled into the car and headed down the road, unsure where to go. It was black outside, only the headlights lighting the way. In the rearview mirror, he saw the lights from the house go dark. Approaching the bridge, Eddie's foot had been on the floor since he left the house. Only now did he let up—too slow for the corners and the bridge. Caroline's eyes watched out for animals, telling him to slow down at times. They came to the bridge, a white light glowing under it, pointing in one direction.

"What is that under the bridge?" She asked as they crossed over it.

"I don't know?" Eddie muttered.

One hand on the wheel and the other dug into his coat pocket. Something was poking him in the side. His fingers curled around a torn scrap of a folded newspaper clipping. He pulled it free. Glancing at it while still driving.

He read the headline, one eye trained on the road, the other on the clipping. Eddie let off the gas, the car slowed, then stopped. Eyes glued to the paper. His hands trembling. His eyes didn't leave the page, reading every word, seeming to read it more than once.

From the back seat, Joey's voice broke the silence

"Dad? What is it? What's wrong?"

The paper in his hand read.

The Stonewall Times

Your Trusted Source for Local News Since 1889

FRONT PAGE:
"TRAGIC ACCIDENT ON LAKE ROAD!"
Stonewall, December 4, 1959

A devastating single-vehicle accident occurred last night on Lake Road, resulting in one fatality. The vehicle reportedly veered off the winding road, plummeted down an embankment, and rolled three times before erupting into flames. Authorities have launched an immediate investigation into the cause. Several residents reported sightings of deer near the road just moments before the crash.

DAY 2 HEADLINE:
"VICTIM IDENTIFIED IN LAKE ROAD CRASH"
Stonewall, December 6, 1959

The victim of yesterday's horrific accident on Lake Road has been identified as Caroline Matters, beloved owner of Hotchpot Depot. Ms. Matters was the sole occupant of the vehicle. The accident occurred shortly after dusk. Witnesses reported a plume of smoke rising from the ravine, prompting immediate emergency calls. Fire and rescue crews responded swiftly, but the car was fully engulfed upon their arrival. Despite their best efforts, Caroline Matters could not be saved. She is survived by her devoted husband, Eddie Matters, and their son, Joey Matters.
The community mourns the loss of a respected and cherished figure.

DAY 5: HEADLINE

"FUNERAL SERVICES FOR CAROLINE MATTERS ANNOUNCED"
Stonewall, December 6, 1959

Funeral services for the late Caroline Matters are scheduled for **Friday, December 18, 1959, at 12:00 P.M.**
The ceremony will be held at **Hopewell Baptist Church, 5598 NW 178th Street**.
Edmond, Oklahoma

The public is welcome to attend, offering friends, family, and neighbors the chance to gather, remember, and grieve.

A reception will follow the service.

Eddie sat there, the newspaper clipping slipping from his fingers to the floor of the car. He glances over to Caroline. The seat sits empty; she was never there. Eddie drops the other hand from the wheel. Joey is still calling from the back seat. He turns at look back to Joey. Who's looking back at him with a concerned look on his face? Eddie says nothing, turning back, seeing the empty passenger seat, then staring out the windshield. Eddie sits in silence and eases back on the gas, going down the road again.

Chapter Twelve:
Where the Tracks End
September 24, 1959

𝒟awn of a new day broke, yet it brought little solace. Nearly a month had passed since the unspeakable horror at their house, a night that had etched itself onto their souls. Seeking refuge, Joey and Eddie had fled to the ranch, but sleep remained an elusive dream. How could it be otherwise, with the images of that night burned into their minds? Caroline was gone, with no memory of what happened to her beyond the clipping he had in his hands. Was this all a dream? He was unsure now.

The next morning, leaving Joey safely at the ranch, Eddie returned to the house, driven by a gnawing need for answers. Outside, a baffling normalcy greeted him: trees swayed gently, bushes stood undisturbed, everything as it should be. With bated breath, Eddie stepped inside. The house, impossibly, seemed pristine.

"How can this be?" Eddie said out loud to himself, his voice laced with disbelief, as he stared at the closet door, in perfect condition, so unlike the previous night of terror. He searched, confused, finding nothing else

amiss. The contradiction hung heavy in the air. After a long, disquieting silence, he retreated, collected Joey, and headed directly to the Pastor.

Pastor Hendrix was waiting for them both outside the church, as if he had somehow sensed their impending arrival. They recounted the harrowing events of that frightful night; their voices hushed with lingering fear. The Pastor listened gravely, then advised them to stay somewhere truly safe for a while, promising to visit their house later that day to assess the situation. Eddie and Joey returned to their home under the Pastor's watchful gaze, gathering their belongings. They went back to the ranch, staying for what felt like an eternity, until Pastor Hendrix's call finally came: it was safe to return.

As their car approached their home, they saw Pastor Hendrix and several other solemn figures gathered around the house. This was new, an unexpected sight. The Pastor was chanting, his voice low and rhythmic, repeating words they had never heard before – an ancient, foreign rhythm that seemed to hum in the very air.

"I don't know what Pastor's doing, but it keeps working!" Eddie murmured to Joey; his

115

eyes fixed on the scene. "But what is he saying this time?"

An ancient, foreign rhythm: "Dang-sin-ui yeong-hon-eun ee-sip-sa-il-jjae doe-neun nal i jip-e bal-eul deu-ri-neun sun-gan gal-gi-gal-gi jjij-gyeojil geos-im-ni-da. Eo-dum-i mo-du-reul jip-eo-sam-kil geos-i-myeo, geu eo-tteon tal-chul-gu-do eop-seul geos-im-ni-da."

Pastor Hendrix chanted this repeatedly, circling the house, then finally addressing them, his voice calm amidst the strange words, assuring them it was safe to enter. The other figures nodded to the Pastor, then dispersed to their cars. Eddie stopped the Pastor before he left.

"Pastor, what were you all chanting?" He asked, a tremor in his voice.

"It's the same old language I used before, but this one is more powerful, Eddie." The Pastor explained, his gaze distant, as if seeing beyond them. "It's a prayer we must recite to help you. We must say this repeatedly until we are off your land. Don't worry, Joey, Eddie, this will help you both." He offered a reassuring nod, his voice still measured, as he continued the incantation, walking steadily to his car.

Weeks drifted away. Eddie repaired the

Dream Away Sunrise

house's eaves where the tree had fallen. Life
slowly, steadily, returned to a semblance of
normal. Nothing happened. Eddie even
managed to host the party Joey had so longed
for. Everything, once again, felt perfect.

On the 24th of September. Eddie and
Joey were engrossed in their work, the roads
outside seeming busier, the distant hum of
traffic louder than usual. Joey was at school,
Friday, bringing with it the promise of the
weekend. He was excited to return home,
finish his chores, and rest before playing with
friends the next day. Eddie dreamt of fishing;
The day unfolded with ordinary rhythms. Eddie
picked up Joey from school, decided to eat out,
visited a few friends, taking just enough time to
get home and resume their nightly routine.

As they pulled up to the driveway to
house, a figure materialized just off to the side,
indistinct in the fading light. As they drew
nearer, it shimmered and vanished. It was
nearly 6:00 PM when they finally reached
home.

"Is that Pastor? Over there?" Eddie
asked, peering through the windshield.

Joey squinted, trying to make out the
shape. "I... I don't know... I can't tell." By the
time their car rolled to a stop, the figure was

gone.

"I'll walk around the house and see if it's him. Joey, can you start your chores?" Eddie instructed.

"Okay." Joey replied, already jogging towards the workshop for feed.

Eddie circled to the side of the house, seeing nothing. He continued to the back, his gaze sweeping the ground. He found strange tracks; unlike any animal or human print he knew. He pressed on to the other side of the house, turning the corner. Then he saw something: a dark, indistinct shape. It was looking through the kitchen window.

"Pastor? Is that you?" Eddie called out, his voice wavering slightly.

The figure vanished. A wave of ice-cold dread washed over his arms and neck. He walked to where it had stood, peering into the dark house, but saw nothing amiss. His eyes dropped to the ground.

"*What the hell*?" Eddie muttered under his breath. The same strange tracks were there, but they abruptly ended. Just like the figure, they simply ceased, stopping at the window.

"Dad? Is everything okay?" Joey called out, his voice a distant comfort.

"Um... Yeah, I think so!" Eddie yelled back, forcing a lightness he didn't feel. "I'll be right there." He turned, walking back towards him. *"I don't think I'll tell him about this... not now... not with what we've been through. The Pastor was just here. We should be fine, he thought, trying to convince himself."*

"Sorry, what's that, Dad?" Joey asked as he approached.

"Oh... nothing. Just talking to myself." He lied smoothly, still confused. "Anyway, I didn't see anything. Maybe it was a shadow from the bush over there or something. I didn't see anything."

"Joey, are you about done?"

"Yes! I'll be in shortly, I've got two more things to do, and I'll be in." Turning back to his task.

"Okay, come in and clean up, get ready for bed so you're rested and ready to go tomorrow!" Eddie said, turning to walk towards the house. Joey heard him enter, the door clicking shut behind him. He turned to feed the last of the chickens, then stopped. A subtle wind, blowing towards the house. He scanned his surroundings. It wasn't strong, just a consistent breeze, enough to sway branches but too gentle to make a sound. He scattered

the last of the feed and hurried to finish his
other chore.

The breeze strengthened, almost
imperceptibly. He glanced at the house. It was
still dark inside. Odd, he thought, his dad
should have at least one light on. Ten minutes
passed, and the wind steadily intensified, but
there was no sound to be heard.

"What is going on here..." Joey
mumbled, unheard.

He turned and began walking towards
the house. As he neared, a profound
uneasiness settled over him. He stopped dead.
Wait, I've felt like this before, he thought,
racking his memory. *Ah, this is what I felt when
we first moved here.* The sense of dread
enveloped him. He stood feet from the porch;
an instinct urged him to step back and look up.
He took a few quick steps backward, his gaze
sweeping the house. Nothing seemed amiss
on the first floor. His eyes ascended to the
second. Something was in the window, looking
down at him. It vanished, swift as a shadow.
He rubbed his eyes, looked back up.

"Dad?" He whispered, seeing his father
there, motioning for him to come inside. Joey
blinked, rubbed his eyes again, and looked
back. His dad was still there, waving him in.

Joey stared, then began moving towards the porch again. He took the two steps up to the deck, reached for the doorknob. It was icy cold, too cold, then suddenly warm. He froze for a second before twisting the knob, opening the door, and stepping inside.

Once inside, the sound of the wind outside was now howling, followed by crashes and shattering sounds.

"Dad! Where are you?" Joey called out, his voice swallowed by the storm outside. No reply. He searched the first floor, but he was nowhere to be seen. He kept calling, his voice growing desperate, as he started up the stairs, still unable to hear anything over the cacophony. A window shattered on the first floor.

"*Is this a tornado?*" He thought, his mind racing.

Terrified, he ran to the top of the steps and stopped, peering down the hall. Standing there, he saw his dad.

"Dad!" He cried, relief flooding him.

"Oh, hey. Come here." Eddie said, his voice eerily peaceful, softly calm.

He walked towards him. "Dad, I've been calling for you! What's happening?"

"Oh, sorry. I didn't hear you." Turning to

look out the window. "Come here, and look!" He added.

Joey walked to the window. Through the sounds of breaking glass and splintering wood, he saw only oppressive darkness outside. The faint light filtering through the window revealed trees bending violently towards the house, some snapped in half, others already collapsed onto the roof.

"DAD, what is going on?" Joey cried out, his voice cracking.

He turned, the sounds of destruction now coming from inside the home. More windows exploding inward, the very structure of the house groaning, tearing itself apart. Eddie moved Joey away from the window just before it shattered, shards of glass showering the floor. A violent rush of wind tore through the room. Then, they heard it: a deep, resonant droning from outside, steadily growing louder. They retreated down the stairs to the center of the living room, their backs to the staircase.

The droning swelled, and a dark red light began to pulsate on the ceiling, bleeding down from above. It flickered erratically, then, abruptly, silence. The red glow persisted, but the wind had stopped.

"What is going…?" Joey began, his

voice trailing off.

A sudden, heavy stomping echoed from the floor above. Back and forth it went, growing louder, heavier. They backed away from the staircase. Eddie glanced up, seeing nothing but the steps, still strangely intact. As the stomping reached the edge of the second-floor landing, a deafening BOOM! reverberated through the house. Explosions ripped through the upper floor, continuous and violent. Before they could reach the front door, a part of a blown-apart body landed in front of them, grotesque and terrifying, then vanished into nothingness. Another explosion rocked the house, beams splintering, sections of the ceiling collapsing. Eddie shoved Joey towards the kitchen. Something whipped past them. *Part of a tree?* Eddie thought, his mind reeling.

"Why us? Why is this happening to us? What did we do?" Joey cried out, his voice raw with terror.

Eddie stood fast, his mind a frantic scramble for the next move. The red light flashed, now intercut with blinding white, as more explosions tore through the house. An arm, clad in a greenish-tan uniform, flew past Eddie's face. He instinctively ducked, the severed limb streaking by. He squeezed his eyes shut, the sounds now deafening: more explosions, pops, the sharp splintering of wood. When he opened them, the wind and trees outside were visible, *despite* the flashing, chaotic lights from within the house.

"Run!" Eddie bellowed. "Run!" He repeated, his voice hoarse, as he watched trees outside being ripped from the ground, pulled inexorably towards the house. But even as he spoke, something seized Joey, dragging him across the floor, then yanking him into the air towards the house's center.

The house itself seemed to be collapsing inward, folding in on itself. Eddie had no choice but to bolt for the door. The thought of leaving Joey behind was a fresh agony; sheer terror for his own life consumed him. Another explosion, a violent shift, and the house contorted inwards from all sides. He glanced back for Joey, but he had vanished.

Eddie grabbed the doorknob, and an agonizing, searing burn coursed through his veins. He squeezed his eyes shut in pain. An overwhelming crash echoed in his ears, a blinding white light searing through his eyelids. He closed his eyes tighter, inhaling a deep, shuddering breath, wondering if it would be his last.

Dream Away Sunrise

Chapter Thirteen:
The Beginning of The End
September 25, 1959

*E*ddie woke to the sound of screaming tires and twisting metal.

The night was bitterly cold under the bridge. Flickers of orange light danced across the concrete above him. He sat up stiffly, clutching a tattered blanket around his shoulders, his back and legs aching from the hard ground. In the near distance, the remains of a wrecked car burned beneath the overpass, one headlight still glowing dimly in the smoke.

The dream was gone. Caroline was gone. Joey too. The warmth, the memories, the illusion—gone. All of it... They were never real. Not here. Not now. Just echoes of a life he never got to live.

He crawled from the drainage tube— once built as a tornado shelter—now filling with smoke. Staggering to his feet, he stumbled at first but soon caught his balance, shuffling down the embankment toward the road. The fire had overtaken the car. Amidst the rising flames, Eddie saw the figure of a small child wandering nearby.

Flashbacks hit him like shrapnel.

Sergeant Eddie Matters was born on October 21, 1932, in Henryetta, Oklahoma. He enlisted in the Army when the Korean War broke out in 1950 and served a brutal three-year tour that left more than just physical scars.

He grew up in Henryetta—just over an hour from Shawnee, two and a half from Oklahoma City—though that city always felt farther than the map suggested. He still remembered Hopewell Baptist Church, the striking structure he once attended, its architecture notable enough to win awards.

One jungle ambush wiped out half his unit. Eddie stepped into a booby trap. Later, he took multiple rounds of gunfire and shrapnel while dragging men to safety, bleeding the whole way. For his actions, he was awarded multiple medals, including two Purple Hearts.

His body has mostly healed. His mind never did.

In the final weeks of the war, Eddie lay near death in a Korean field hospital. His injuries nearly claimed him more than once. But when he finally woke, the first thing he saw was Caroline—a kind-faced nurse with eyes full of warmth. Over the following weeks, they formed a bond in the hospital's haze of pain and morphine. He always remembered the pain. The sting of the IVs, the burn that ran through his hands and arms.

It was there he also met a young boy named Joey—a Korean kid been a real boy once, seven, maybe ten, just a scared kid in the wreckage of a village outside Incheon. Eddie never even knew his last name. He lingered around the camp. Joey spoke more English than anyone expected, and he took to Eddie almost immediately. They became inseparable, even if only for a short time. Eddie remembered Joey's story: how he was found unconscious, hanging from a tree, brought to the hospital by American soldiers. He woke there, unafraid of the Americans, choosing to stay around the camp, eventually calling Eddie his "American Dad."
Pastor Hendrix, the Army chaplain, had read Eddie his last rites. No one thought he'd survive. But somehow, he pulled through, and the chaplain became a companion. They talked often—about war, about God, about what came next.

In the last days of the war, just before he was taken to the field hospital, his unit came under heavy fire. The sky screamed with helicopters and planes with bombs following. Eddie and a handful of others dove for cover wherever they could. He ended up in a larger hut—strongly built, sturdier than most. But it didn't matter. A bomb landed just beyond the far wall, close enough to rip the place open. Wood, fire, and pieces of men flew past him. He was lucky. He made it out. But survival didn't mean clarity. His body had escaped, but his mind stayed locked in that hut—frozen, crouched, waiting to die.

A week before Eddie was to be discharged, he received terrible news. Caroline had been killed—gunned down in an ambush while riding in a convoy. The vehicle had tumbled down a ravine after the attack; everyone inside perished. Eddie never forgot that day. He buried the pain deep, locking it away inside his already fractured mind.

Two days later, the hospital itself came under attack. Bombs rained down. Deafening blasts rocked the compound. Eddie watched in horror as Chaplain Hendrix ran for cover, only to be swallowed by a sudden flash of fire and light. Gone in an instant. A moment Eddie could never unseen. Then, just as quickly as it began, the assault ended.

Eddie stood frozen, shell-shocked. Around him, chaos. Then Joey appeared, running toward him with a man through the smoke and the screams. They checked him for wounds, but Eddie couldn't speak. Couldn't move. The man rushed off to help others, but Joey stayed by his side, sobbing.

The next morning, a helicopter came to evacuate the boy and a few others. Eddie watched them lift into the sky, his face blank, his heart hollow. It was a hard goodbye. Joey was sent to a safer village, and Eddie often wondered what became of him, hoping he had found a real life, far from war and memory.

Later that day, another chopper arrived to take Eddie and several soldiers back to the States.

Back in Oklahoma, Eddie spent time recovering before moving back in with his father, Vinnie, on the family ranch. The house he returned to was the home he grew up in. He and his father rebuilt it together—piece by piece—adding the woodshed, the workshop, every beam a memory. The home was beautiful, strong, and custom-built by their hands. A few years later, his father passed away, leaving Eddie the house—and the silence.

But Eddie's condition never improved. Shell shock—what they now call PTSD— fractured his thoughts and haunted his nights.

The war never left him. It lurked in his dreams, his shadows, his silence. Nightmares consumed him. His mental health spiraled. Unfit for work, he drifted into homelessness. Moving from place to place, finding shelter wherever he could. Seeking comfort in people he used to know, in places long gone. He feared sleep. It always brought the war back.

Flashbacks taunted him. Shadows of people that resembled those from the war triggered terrifying episodes. He heard voices in Korean, real or imagined. Phrases from his nightmares:

- "Ulineun dangsin-ui kkum-eseo dangsin-eul jab-eul geos-ibnida." ("We will catch you in your dreams.")
- "Ee Jip-Gwa ee sa-ram-deul-eh-geh chook-bok-eul nae-ree-shi-go, ee-got-eh een-neun mo-ak-han gi-oon-eun-sa-ra-ji-geh ha-so-seo." ("Please bless this house and these people, and make any evil energy here disappear.")
- "I jibi dangsin-deurui yeonghon-eul ppaeatgo, amugeotdo namgiji ankireul." ("May this house steal your souls and leave nothing behind.")

- "Dang-sin-ui yeong-hon-eun ee-sip-sa-il-jjae doe-neun nal i jip-e bal-eul deu-ri-neun sun-gan gal-gi-gal-gi jjij-gyeojil geos-im-ni-da. Eo-dum-i mo-du-reul jip-eo-sam-kil geos-i-myeo, geu eo-tteon tal-chul-gu-do eop-seul geos-im-ni-da." ("Your soul will be torn to shreds the moment you set foot in this house on the twenty-fourth day. Darkness will engulf everyone, and there will be no escape.")

Were they spoken to him? Or created by a broken mind? He couldn't tell anymore.

One morning, Eddie saw a Korean man outside a store. The man said nothing, but the sight of him pulled Eddie back to the war. One of many faces. One of many choices. Kill or be killed. Eddie had never recovered from the first life he took. The guilt never let him go. The pain, physical and emotional, still haunted him.

He often felt the wounds on his chest as if they were fresh. Sharp as blades, always there. The hospitals had done what they could, but no stitches could repair a shattered soul.

He also recalled a cold winter day in his youth, when he'd accidentally driven his car off the road and crashed into a river. He'd had to walk a bit to his dad's house to get warmed up again. His dad had been angry, but seeing the wreckage, he'd somewhat forgiven him, understanding it wasn't entirely his fault. The cold never helped him much, always leading to flashbacks of the heat from explosions around him. He neither cared for the heat nor the cold much these days.

In his days back in the States, before homelessness consumed him, he had tried going to church. He'd seen a few pastors, all of whom tried their best to help him. They would sit and listen to his stories, some of which they could barely stand to hear, but they listened and tried to give peace to the man.

He remembered everything: the battles, the explosions, the confusion, the screams. Soldiers on both sides scrambling to survive. Chaos, blood, fire. The worst of humanity. His mind, desperate to protect itself, invented dreams—kind ones—where Caroline still lived. Where Joey laughed. Where the home stood tall and safe.

But dreams could never protect him. Not from the truth. Not from the war. Not from himself. He was a troubled man, haunted by all he could never let go.

From the burning wreckage he turns,

knowing he cannot help the victims in the car—the figure he saw was nothing more than a fleeting hope. He stoops to pick up the worn blanket that had slipped from his shoulders, pulls it tight against the morning chill, and keeps walking down the road. Joey's laughter echoes in his mind as the sun rises behind him, spilling light over the dark. Another dream gone. Another sunrise to face. He walks on, in search of the next place to lay his head. And then the story begins again.

About the Author

Mike Rivera was born in Glenwood Springs, Colorado, and grew up in the town of Rifle, Colorado. He now lives back in Glenwood Springs with his wife, Amanda, and their talkative parakeet, Cicero.

Dream Away Sunrise began in 2020, sparked by Mike's frustration with the repetitive tropes in modern horror—same plot, different title. Craving something more authentic and emotionally resonant, he set out to write a story that felt real.

Drawing from his own life, Mike wove together fragments of vivid dreams, memories of his grandfather's time in the Korean War, and character names from skits by the likes of George Carlin and Brian Regan. Many of the book's settings and dates are rooted in real places—some you can even look up—giving the story an unsettling sense of realism.

For Mike, this book was never about jump scares. It was about uncovering truth hidden in plain sight.

Dream Away Sunrise
A Psychological Novella of Horror

They moved into the house on a Friday. By Saturday, the hallway had footsteps of its own.

In the rolling foothills of rural Oklahoma, Eddie thought he'd found peace: a house to fix, a woodshed to raise, A wife and a boy who still believed monsters weren't real. Mornings brought sunrise. Nights brought silence. And something else.

The old house breathes. It remembers. It keeps secrets.

And Eddie? He's trying not to remember anything at all.

Dream Away Sunrise is a quiet American psychological thriller, where nothing is quite what it seems—and the real horror lives in the spaces no one talks about.

Dream Away *Sunrise*